# CHICO'S WOMEN

# CHICO'S WOMEN

MARCH HASTINGS

CUTTING EDGE

ISBN-13: 978-1-954840-86-7

Published by
Cutting Edge Books
PO Box 8212
Calabasas, CA 91372
www.cuttingedgebooks.com

# CHAPTER ONE

"**D**ON'T TEMPT me, George."

"But, Carol, *you?*"

"And why not me?" she said lightly and turned to lift the bubbling kettle from the stove beside them.

"I don't know .... I thought women like you didn't."

She heard the cautious pause and the creak of wooden chair legs as he leaned back against the kitchen wall.

"Didn't what, dear?" she said. Didn't have the courage? Or didn't find him attractive? In five short years, Jonny Chico had become a romantic legend. All women found him attractive. And why shouldn't she, married to a man like George?

A flick of anger licked across her lips. Why was he pushing her? Why couldn't he let their marriage rest in peace like the cold corpse it was? Her glance darted upward through the double windows to the brisk sky blowing scraps of cloud across the world. How lovely to be out there. To wander and roam without thought.

Quietly, she poured the tea into the silver pot and set it beside their two cups on the server. Everything in place. Sugar, cream, linen napkins, toast tray. The order of their days strung out like tarnished beads on the heavy noose of their life together. She could tell him a few things. How dull it was. Everything dull. Brunch and lunch and tea. Who could care about pretty details when everything came through so soggy, so tasteless? And their so-called love-making mixed in with it all, just as bland and habitual.

"I'll do that," he said.

She stepped ahead and let him push the tray into the livingroom. *I ought to let it pass,* she thought. *It's not a safe topic for married people to talk about.*

"George, let's not stay home this evening."

"Oh?"

Pressed by an urgency stronger than logic, Carol leaned forward and touched his wrist. "Let's forget about tea and television and Paterson's party. Let's go some place. Just the two of us."

She felt him watching her, the wide gray eyes sharp with curiosity. He seemed to hold and probe her with his gaze, as though she were a specimen on one of the slides beneath his microscope.

"This is news," he said.

"Is it?" A sudden helplessness descended. How could she feel so little, so lost for the right words?

"Yes, wouldn't you say so? There we were, talking about Jonny Chico until you positively began to drool and now you want to go out with me. Alone. What's eating you anyway, Carol? Got the seven year bug between your legs?"

She felt her cheeks go hot with flame.

"You know what I think?" Calmly, he lifted a teacup and settled down into the high pillowed sofa. "I think you're afraid, my dear wife. I think you're afraid to meet Jonny Chico face to face and that's why you don't want to go to the party tonight." Casually, he lifted his legs and crossed them on the cushions.

"No," she said, struggling to keep her own voice even. "You're making things up again. Trying to force me into one of your pet theories. But it isn't true, George. And I'm not a specimen in your laboratory."

"Sit down, my sweet, and don't aggravate yourself. I don't really care if you do have a thing for him. All the women do. It's his profession, after all. So why should you be an exception to the ravages of his charm?"

Carol watched him lifting a cup of tea toward her but she couldn't take it. Her cold, damp hands trembled within the folds of her skirt. If he would only lose his temper. Explode just once. Get it out and done with. But not George. He had to grind her down slowly, gently. Wear her away year after year. Imperceptibly almost.

"Come, take it," he said. "You need something warm to straighten out those nerves." With his free hand, he patted her knee. "Get you in shape for this evening."

Carol sighed. The anger she had felt in such a hot flash melted into a tepid futility. She couldn't talk to him any more. Perhaps they never had understood each other, really.

She accepted the cup and sipped slowly at the sweetish, diluted cream. "I can't let you go on thinking about me that way," she persisted.

"What way?"

She glanced at him quickly. The long, thin face had compressed into a round innocence. "You know."

"But, dearest, I don't."

"All right then. You didn't do anything." The cup clattered lightly on its saucer. "You didn't say or imply anything. I made it up. It's all my fault." Her voice rose to a treble of desperation. "I'm sorry."

"Sorry for what, my love?"

Carol set the cup down on the tray with a slam and strode toward the whisky cabinet. "That you had the godawful misfortune to marry a whore."

At the far end of the living room she felt miles away from him—separated by furniture and pretense and bitterness. With unconscious strength, she twisted free the cork from a new bottle of Scotch and splashed some into a tall glass. She could run from room to room, lock herself away at the farthermost end of their vast apartment. But liquor was the only real way she could escape him.

"Carol, please."

One large hand cupped her shoulder, holding her tight.

"Leave me be." Her voice was low, a mere grunt, animal-like in its mute misery.

"I didn't mean to upset you."

She drank the whisky fast, before he could take the glass away. "I'm tired," she said finally. "Just plain tired. Maybe we ought to get a divorce, George. Nothing I do ever seems to make a difference with you any more."

His hand turned her to face him. With one crooked finger he tilted her chin gently upward. "You don't mean that. You're angry and overwrought and I don't blame you. It's been a hard day. Everything's been going wrong at that damned lab for two weeks now and I come home and take it out on you. You're an angel for being so patient with me."

The words banged like tin inside her head. She'd heard them before. All of them. With the same appeal for forgiveness. She let him kiss her lightly on the mouth, then rest the side of her face against his shoulder. It was how he had held her in the old days when they'd had something worthwhile together. But now it was just an act. A farce. She wondered why he bothered.

"Maybe you're right about just the two of us going out."

His words wafted over her head. She didn't answer him. Why exert herself when it didn't really matter where they went or when or what happened when they got wherever they were going?

"It's all right," she said. "Paterson is expecting us. I was only being impulsive."

She felt the hard block of his chest begin to relax. He needed to go to the party. Keep old man Paterson on tap for an endowment next year. No matter what else happened in his life, George always managed to sew up the loose ends of his research with good, substantial money. And Tom Paterson was an admirable source of supply. Always bored, always restless, he used his money to buy himself kicks. Perhaps that was why he had decided to back Jonny Chico's new television show. And perhaps that, too, had led him to give a party in Chico's honor.

Carol closed her eyes for an instant and resigned herself to the evening's mayhem. There was no fighting it.

The whisky began to seep gently downward, spreading peace. Yes, why not go to the party and enjoy herself? Old man Paterson had a strange taste in people—collected them for the odd quirks in their personalities like weird growths of crystal. Even without Chico, the evening should prove amusing. With him, anything might happen.

"I ought to be getting dressed," she whispered and tried very subtly to move out of George's grasp.

His mouth touched her forehead. "There's time."

The touch of his breath on her scalp made Carol pause. He was going to try it again. Try to make love to her. Whenever they argued, he needed to possess her. Reassure himself by climbing inside her body. Perhaps convince his sceptical brain that she was still there. All of her. Giving none of herself away to anyone else. Or anything.

"I love you," he said.

She didn't have to reply. Merely stand there. Allow his fingers to graze down along her back and slip over the curve of her behind.

"I love you, Carol. Very much."

She could not move away now. His palms pressed against her buttocks, holding her in tight against him. Her own arms drooped at her sides. She felt oddly silly. Like an ape, with her arms hanging like that. She lifted them around his neck.

"Do you?"

She heard the quick intake of breath and felt the hard rise of his maleness. The pressure against her sprung a secret latch that released a wild hope in her. Perhaps this once he meant it. Perhaps, in his own selfish way, he did love her. Maybe this brand of passion was the best George had to give.

Impulsively her arms tightened around his neck. She lifted her hips to meet the searching of him. Of all the things in life she knew, George's body she knew best of all. Why question? *Take what he has to give you and be grateful.*

"I need you," she whispered against his earlobe, wanting to encourage, hoping to smooth away the last lingering barbs of anger.

She felt his lips widening into a smile against her temple.

They moved backward among the tables and chairs until George pulled her down with him onto the couch.

"It's good here," he said, "with the sun on you."

A warm, ruddy light spilled over her caressingly as his fingers unfastened her clothing. The expert movements reminded her how many times George had undressed her, touched her, owned her. She felt the sweet-hard suction of his mouth on her breast and closed her eyes.

Her own hands moved now, searching to cup his head and press him even harder to her flesh. She found the naked, hard shoulder, the bulging compactness of his arm. Her nails dug into his skin and she lifted herself to him.

Impulsively, she cradled him between her knees, turning sideways against the back of the couch, rocking him within the hammock of her limbs.

"Love me, darling...." Her words were soft, yet painful with a need to preserve the moment.

His body hunched over her, demanding, possessive. The rough angle of his chin bruised along her soft flesh, scraping here and there the side of one breast, the line of a rib, a curve of belly. Beneath him she felt tiny. Tiny, yet gorged with lust.

His tongue darted and touched, urging her, goading her. She realized how well he knew the map of her pleasure. And how he would explore every bypath, explode every nerve, irritate every quivering muscle until she trembled on the point of wildness.

The edges of his teeth caught the inside of one thigh and she twisted toward him.

"Not yet," he said on the crest of a chuckle. "Not till you're dying for me."

Her fingers groped blindly. She found the slim line of his hips and grasped him. Her palms slipped on the film of their own perspiration. All thought slid away. A great gulf of tension vibrated through her, around her, consuming her brain. At last her body lifted for him, pleading.

She felt him lower with a sudden movement.

*If it could always be like this... together.*

"George..." The breath gasped through her tense jaw. "...darling." Carol heard her own voice as though from across the universe. She seemed to be spinning away, her belly whirling in a maelstrom of desire. She clung to him tight with all her limbs, galloping on the rhythm of her need....

... Carol lay half off the couch, the weight of one breast sliding forward. Quiet abandon rested beneath her flesh. Her eyelids drooped with the weight of slumber.

The sweet odor of a fresh cigarette reached her nostrils. She pulled herself up on the couch to watch George. He sat pressed into the fartherest corner of the couch, a cigarette dangling from the sharpened angles of his face. He had receded a thousand miles from their love-making, she knew. Returned, without wasting a minute, to thoughts of the only world that really interested him. Carol sat back with a sigh. "All right," she said brightly, lightly from behind the mask again. "We'd better get dressed for the party."

# CHAPTER TWO

EVERYONE HAD heard about Jonny Chico. Men smiled to themselves about him. Girls tittered. And nice women wouldn't admit what they knew.

Carol tried not to think about him as she dressed. And yet, she had never been truly able to stop thinking about him. Not since they were kids together, kids in love. She had known even then that love with Jonny Chico was more like a disease. And when, at twenty, he had been carted off to jail for pimping, she had tried to forget him. She hadn't written or gone to visit. And by the time of his release five years ago, she had already met and married George. Yet she could never forget Chico. He was always there. Posing now as a health specialist to cover up his less legitimate activities. A big name in the entertainment field, respected, idolized and adored by millions of women. In the limelight always.

No, she couldn't forget Jonny Chico. And yet she dared not remember.

With the door closed against George, she must proceed to gather her poise. Tonight she would need it.

She turned on the radio till she found the persuasive guitar music that helped relax her, then carried it into the bathroom and set it on one corner of the wide porcelain tub. The ornate bathroom irked her. Of what use the dolphin shaped faucets and marble flooring when George needed money so badly for his work? But she had learned not to question his fantastic need for display. Instead, she ran the water and settled herself beneath the high swaying foam, letting the warmth mingle with the music in a soothing ointment against her despair.

Yet, even with her eyes closed, she could not quite push away the image of her husband trying to placate her with sex instead of love. The painful knowledge brought her into action and she began to scrub her body as though by sheer energy she could rub off the futility of his touch.

Afterward, she chose from the line of dresses in her crowded closet a simple black one that clung.

He might not love her, but he demanded to be proud of her appearance. In this one way, at least, Carol knew she did not disappoint him. She could walk into a room or merely stand still or even be sitting … she could do nothing more than merely exist and through the crowd George would glance at her his gleam of approval. The years of dance training had formed her well. Made of her a display he was proud of. Like their ten-room apartment.

The thoughts would not stop. They peopled her mind with nervous company as she hooked herself into the new, single piece of black lace that molded her shape from breast downward through the line of her full hips. Carefully, she worked at the full dark coil of her hair, then twisted it high on the crown of her head and attached the sparkling tiara that seemed to light her deep eyes with the life that she did not feel.

Who could care about Jonny Chico? Who could give a damn about somebody who couldn't help her? She needed a genie, an elf, a fairy godmother to touch George with a magic wand and transform him back to the man she had fallen in love with and married. Her chest ached with a yearning for those days. They had meant something to each other then. They had fed each other strength and encouragement. There had been laughter between them and quiet understanding. And for a while, George had erased the specter of Jonny Chico from her mind.

Where had it all gone? When had the luster of their mariage begun to fade to the dull patina of tedium? George's work, his ambition had come between them, widening each year the gap in their relationship. If only once he thought of her before the lab. If only once…

The gold clock on the mantle began to chime. Seven o'clock tinkled gracefully into her life. She sprayed a touch of perfume into the deep well of her bosom, then strolled out to face George as though the afternoon had never happened.

She touched the doorknob of his bedroom and pushed it gently.

"Are you ready?" she said as the door swung open.

"A minute."

He stood at the mirror of his dresser, head tilted, brushing with the initialed silver brush the hair that seemed always neatly combed anyhow. Carol stood in the doorway and folded her arms, waiting. She hated this room, his privacy, the never-ending thoughts that kept him from her.

"You look ravishing," she said, letting a touch of mockery into her tone.

"Thanks."

His lips pursed for an instant, but he wouldn't pick a fight. Not now. Not before the party. He wouldn't risk any ruffled feelings for Paterson or any of the others to detect.

He came toward her and kissed her lightly on the cheek. His touch was like the touch of butterfly wings, a token of his expectancy that she fly beautifully for him tonight.

"Ready?" he said.

He took her fur wrap and set it on her shoulders. The soft, white ermine set off the deep mystery of black and Carol felt grateful that she could gain at least this one fleeting scrap of approval from George. If she could hang onto this, perhaps… perhaps some day he would see deeper into the meaning of their marriage.

And it was this hope that made her persist, cling, and take each moment with hope. It had been good for them once. So perfect. And it could be like that again, if he truly loved her, if he began to see her again as a woman and not just an adjunct of his ambition. She knew that what she had shared with George could not really be destroyed.

They rode quietly together down from their penthouse to the lighted canopy and Park Avenue. A first touch of autumn snapped at coat tails and ruffled the fur of small dogs bouncing by. She waited, heard the doorman blowing his shrill whistle for their cab and nodded greeting to a group of neighbors just coming in. Little touches that told her she still belonged in the world; had not floated away, as George was doing, into self-absorption.

In the taxi, they both lit cigarettes. A gesture of companionship on Carol's part. A final moment of being alone with him before the curtain went up on his show.

And then, almost before she knew it, George was ringing the bell of the house on Fifth Avenue. A wide, remodeled building, substantial, sandblasted white, young somehow with cheerfully brightened windows and the sound of lively voices trickling through to them.

It was only eight o'clock but already the entrance foyer was filled with many coats and furs. The tangy odor of Paterson's Italian tobacco hovered like a welcome.

"Let's go in," George said low in her ear. "He'll find us."

Carol heard the slight tremble in George's voice. As though he weren't quite certain. An instant of pity flashed through her.

"I'm sure he'll be looking for us," she said with a burst of sincerity. He needed her. She knew George needed her. And she would always give him whatever she had of love, moral support ... and anything else that he might want.

She took his arm and they proceeded through the wide entrance where blossoms of voices and laughter made a bouquet of animation. For a hairsbreadth, Carol hesitated. She paused to fix the proper smile, the casual enjoyment of living that she always found so useful and that George found so complimentary to himself.

"Well, hello there," a big voice boomed.

"Hello, Riker." George grinned at the bulbous, bespectacled shape lumbering toward them through the crowd.

"My dear Carol."

Carol allowed the big hand to encircle hers and squeeze it, holding on just an instant too long, as the smile he gave her was a trifle too wide, the bulging eyes a trifle too searching for her to feel at ease with this colleague of George's. Yet, with seeming innocence, she smiled up at the double chins and the sparce graying hair.

"Why must I see you only at parties?" he said.

She remained quite poised within the aura of his lilac hair tonic and tilted her head slightly. "Why indeed?" she murmured, wishing George would wangle them free.

"Looking for Paterson?" Riker said as George's face darted back up from a freshly lit cigarette.

"Why not?" George grinned. "He's paying for all this."

Carol wished that his voice had sounded just a little less impressed. Around them waiters moved with trays of glasses and other trays of tidbits. Gloved hands and strong hands and slender hands seemed to be moving to take something or put something down or light another cigarette or touch an uncertain coiffure.

"He's somewhere up near that window," Riker said. "Come along, I'll beat you a path to his door."

"No thanks," George said too quickly.

His voice sounded brittle and Carol said to cover it, "Would someone be good enough to find me a martini?"

"Of course, darling."

George was off through the crowd, leaving her alone with the huge mound of shiny flesh.

"Well, now ..." Riker reached around the shoulder of a uniform and brought a filled glass off the tray. "Good of your husband to leave us alone for a moment."

Carol smiled quietly while she hated Riker behind it for making a fool of George. She did not have to follow George with her gaze to know that he had used her martini as an excuse to go wandering off in search of Paterson. She took the drink from Riker's fingers and raised it to her lips. But she must not gulp it down. She must betray no emotion. No fear. No anger. Only the pleasant, pampered, amused side of Mrs. George Trace. She sipped slowly.

"Now, now, drink it down," Riker's voice urged with mock irritation. "We'll never get friendly this way."

"That, Riker, may be the most interesting facet of our relationship." And Carol nodded blandly as she thought: *bastard.*

She turned slightly away from him, aware that if she did not try to pull in someone else, Riker would eventually manage to get her into a corner. But most of the faces Carol did not recognize.

"The roving eye, my dear Carol?" Riker took a cigar from an inner pocket and cut off the tip with an incisive bite of his front teeth. "George will come back to you eventually." He lifted the tobacco from his tongue and dropped it into an empty glass. "Or are you looking for Mr. Chico?"

Carol remained silent. The strain of seeming good-natured took all her energy.

"You may as well relax, my dear. Mr. Chico hasn't arrived as yet. Or perhaps he is upstairs having a private conversation with one of the ladies."

"Riker, you're too much," Carol burst.

"Ah, yes. But not enough to rival Jonny ...."

"Darling, *sweet* Carol."

Quickly Carol turned to the trilling voice as though welcoming salvation. "Well, Tammy Lynn, of all people."

The young woman shook her bright blonde curls. "Surprised? Surprised to see me at a shindig like this?" She waved a cigarette holder. "I wouldn't have missed such an opportunity for the world. You know what I said? I said to Marvin, Marvin, you've been good for nothing to me for fifteen years, now use your biochemical influence and *get* us to that party." She flicked an ash that drifted down onto Riker's protruding jacket front. "So he did."

A wave of genuine pleasure melted through Carol's tight nerves. "I'm so glad you're here," she breathed. "Oh, yes—this is George's test-tube companion, Riker Granger."

"How do you do, Tammy."

"I didn't think there would be any *men* at *this* party," Tammy waved her white-gloved fingers.

Riker leaned back into his chins. "The male species is represented, my dear lady, out of scientific curiosity, you see. And for décor. Natural masculine chivalry will add a certain obstacle to Mr. Chico's total conquest." He lifted a small sandwich from a passing tray. "Or so it is hoped."

Tammy giggled, revealing unexpected wrinkles of age along her neck. "Instant harem, you mean?"

"Now, Tammy," Carol shook her head.

"Oh, you must just pardon my wild, wild enthusiasm, dearest. It's been years since anything has stirred up my hackles like this. I mean, not since Father Divine."

Riker touched Carol's shoulder. "Don't look so bewildered, my dear. I'm sure George must have taught you something."

His eyes glittered through thick lids, holding her steadily in his observation.

"All right," Carol said. "I give up. Where is he, this irresistible Mr. America?"

"Oh, he's hardly that *healthy*," Tammy's voice went deep.

"I don't care what he is. I just want to see him and get it over with," Carol said, permitting a touch of her impatience to show.

"You'll see him," Riker said slowly. "And I'm sure you will enjoy yourself."

The air was becoming hot and thick with its accumulation of smoke and human exudation. Unashamedly, Carol began to swivel her head, glancing hopefully from group to group in search of George. He had a habit of disappearing when things got tight. Perhaps he had buttonholed Paterson and dragged him off to the library for an impassioned talk about the lab. Involvement with money troubles might lead to anything. If Paterson was giving him a hard time, she might not see George until daybreak.

Gloved fingers grabbed her wrist. "You *must* come with me," Tammy said and began pulling her through the crowd. "You'll excuse us, Mr. Granger won't you?"

Carol allowed herself to be pulled along, glad of even the most clumsy excuse for getting rid of him.

Tammy seemed to swim ahead of her, making a clearing through the couples and groups. When they reached the other side of the room, she paused and took a deep breath. "What a creep, creep, *creep*," Tammy chewed down on her cigarette holder. "I pity poor George having to work with *that*."

Despite herself, Carol smiled.

"He looked like he was going to whip your panties off any instant."

"Now, Tammy, let's not get morbid."

"But that's just what it was, I tell you. But never mind. There's Marvin. See him? The one with the big red ears. His ears always go red when he's embarrassed. I just hope that sweet little thing giving him a line doesn't drop him for dead when Jonny Chico comes in."

Carol's ears closed against the name. She did not want to hear it again. Not ever. The very sound of the words seemed to give off an evil that she did not want to be near. And besides, it had caused a fight with George today. Anything that could cause a fight she wanted to stay far away from. But there was no way of turning Tammy off. And if she floated around the room alone, she might meet up with Riker.

"Carol, you look so blasé. I certainly wish I could hide my excitement as well as you."

Carol took a drink for each of them off one of the passing trays. "Maybe that's because I'm not excited."

She felt free now to drink the whisky down. Though Tammy did a lot of babbling, she was not the kind of person to give away secrets. If the woman sensed her discomfort, she would certainly not pry.

"Then I'm enough so for both of us. Do I sound silly, Carol? A big, grown-up woman talking like a——"

The sudden, odd pause in Tammy's voice alerted Carol. She saw the woman's wide round eyes grow suddenly still. Instinctively, Carol turned to see what she stared at.

At first, she noticed only Paterson, who stood very thin, very tanned and deeply wrinkled beneath the great shock of white hair that rose like a flag of surrender above his aging forehead. Her first thought shot to her heart like a poisoned arrow: *Where's George?* If they weren't in the library together, then where? And doing what?

As this first sense of concern began to tighten in her throat, she kept her eyes on Paterson, watching the chipper, light-hearted openness that made him the number one party-giver in the gossip columns. She felt Tammy's hand squeezing her arm slowly, tightening unconsciously with anxious pleasure.

And there, very grave beside Paterson, taller than any other man in the room and strangely quiet with neither drink nor cigarette, Carol knew stood Jonny Chico.

She had not seen him for years.

They had both been kids. Maybe fifteen, when they met.

And he had changed, she saw, in the way she knew he would have to change. He was smarter—obviously smoother—no more small-time punk.

Her ankles seemed to grow weak as she watched him. They had been only kids. Yet she remembered a feeling shared with him that she could never mention to George. Then, she had called it love. Now she knew other names for what they had had. Jonny had always brought out in her the very basest emotions. And from his phenomenal success, she realized that he affected other women the same way. Touching the gutter part of their souls, churning up a kind of insatiable need that they would not have dreamed themselves capable of. Even speaking to them over the radio as a health specialist, advising them on diets and exercise, his honeyed voice stirred up wildness in the women who listened. Jonny Chico was the embodiment of evil, more a phallic symbol than a man. A satyr who taught lust to bored and lonely women.

And Carol was bored tonight … and lonely. Yet she dared not give in to her desire. Not now.

*I'm safe,* she thought. *He won't remember me. How could he possibly? We've both changed. I even more than he.*

"Look at the way he just stands there," Tammy breathed. "Doesn't it electrify you?"

"Not in the least," Carol said in words that sounded jerky and lame.

Around her the room had grown suddenly quieter. The forced conversation of people with minds on other things sputtered from group to group.

On the surface, Paterson seemed unaware of the impression his guest was making. He took his time about introducing him to the women that managed to wriggle into talking range. And yet, watching him, Carol could almost feel the sparks of his tension. There was pride in his bearing, the pride of having produced a rare entertainment for his party. And there was something else. Revulsion … or was it hatred, perhaps. Carol could not quite catch the nuance of emotion. And yet she sensed a strong antipathy between the two men.

"Come on," Tammy said. "We've got to take the initiative."

"Carol's knees went rigid. "Don't be silly."

"But I am silly."

"Tammy." The tone was meant to chastize.

"I've got to, Carol. You just don't know."

Carol tried to pull free. It was one thing to feel safe at a distance. But why tempt fate by being introduced? No, she couldn't risk it. Even with her different name, her different manner, she couldn't feel satisfied that he wouldn't sense something about her.

"Then you go alone," Carol rasped.

"I can't."

"Oh, go ahead."

"I'll look pushy, Carol. You've got to come with me."

Desperation seemed to give Tammy strength and she tugged at Carol's arm with full force.

How could she escape without looking more a fool than Tammy? No, she mustn't, mustn't give herself away.

*George ... oh, George, where are you now to help me? This one time when I need you. George, please....*

"Why, Tom Paterson, so pleased to be at one of your lovely, *lovely* parties."

With dull dread, Carol listened to Tammy's voice rise on its frothy treble. She held another of the dozens of drinks that were pouring after each other down her gullet and pretended to listen to the meaningless gabble. She had to look at somebody so she glanced across at Paterson. He seemed to be listening attentively to Tammy and yet Carol had the feeling that he was not really hearing her at all. As though he could not for an instant relax in the company of Jonny Chico, but kept his senses attuned to him.

"... Of course I brought Marvin along. Over there, see him? Yes, there, with the red——"

And then, as Carol was beginning to quiet a little, there came, low and quiet beneath the gushing waterfall of Tammy's chatter, a voice. A steady, male voice that said: "Bittersweet? Old friend Bittersweet. I'd never hoped to see you again."

Carol held her breath, then let it free in a long expression of release. After fifteen years, she knew she would have to straighten things out with Jonny Chico at last.

# CHAPTER THREE

H E SEEMED to be coming toward her in a huge and blurred image of doom mixed with desire.

Carol felt a strange whisper of breath along her spine. Gripped in a long, slow shiver, she stood quite still, praying for the sensation to pass. Her brightest smile widened curtainlike over the weird, consuming thrill. "Jonny," she said, her voice soft, "how are you?"

Automatically, she extended her hand in welcome. Inwardly, she steeled herself against his touch. *George, come help me....*

Then Jonny's fingertips grazed her own. Lightly. Hardly at all. And her skin began to burn and freeze alternately as her body seemed to sputter to life once more.

"Oh, you two *know* each other."

The tremolo of Tammy's surprise fluttered above them. Yet Carol felt somehow alone with him, isolated as through the party had dissolved.

"Apparently," Patterson said with hearty pleasure. His forehead wrinkled deeply from raised eyebrows of amusement.

Carol barely heard them. Her rigid gaze would not leave the sharp, angular eyes that seemed to be waiting for some betrayal of her true emotions. She ought to say something casual, anything that would tell him she was a grown woman now, in full control of herself ... finally.

But the black eyes with their hint of crouching cruelty would not let her go. One heavy, arched eyebrow twitched like a panther's tail in the bony forehead. It flung her back into the jungle of torment from which she had worked so hard to escape.

Her lips went cold as she realized that she could not pretend. The mask had become like bits of china falling away to reveal her attraction and her fear.

Chico leaned forward. His palm touched her elbow. "This calls for a celebration, doesn't it?" His wide shoulders intercepted both Tammy and Paterson.

"I suppose it does," she said, keeping her voice soft so that he would not hear her uncertainty.

"Well then …."

Carol felt herself being steered through the crowd. She wanted to protest, to hang on to Tammy as a life-saver that would keep her from drifting out of the remnants of her good sense. But deftly the broad body, so sprawling and easy in its black dinner jacket, carved a path for them across the room.

*I mustn't,* she thought. *It can't start all over again. Not now.*

She stiffened her legs to stop them from hurrying so obediently, so disgracefully agreeable to his whim.

"We can't just walk out," she said lamely.

"Why not?"

Carol hesitated. "Well, it is your party, Jonny. You're the guest of honor." Her chin tilted bravely upward, trying to compel him to be convinced.

Chico grinned. The sharp cheekbones jutted forward. He seemed, for an instant, almost brutal. Then the harshness dissolved, leaving only a luminous warmth glowing in his dark eyes.

"The hell I care," he said.

And Carol knew he meant it. "But I can't," she persisted.

"Why?"

"I simply can't, that's all." She made a final, desperate effort to be strong.

He whirled and stared at her. The knife of his glance seemed to cut through her insistence.

"I asked why not?"

He hadn't raised his voice and yet she felt his persistence tightening.

Carol tried to dig her high, needle sharp heels into the carpet. "It's not polite," she said firmly.

Chico snorted. His full lips pursed for an instant. Then he bent toward her ear and whispered, "Crap."

Carol shivered. He hadn't really changed. Not really at all.

The same wild boy. The same contempt for people and their feelings. The same troubled soul, cocky behind the pain-hardened face.

"Besides," Carol continued, "I don't make it a practice to go running out on my husband."

Now she stood still and steady, waiting to see the effect of her final weapon.

Chico paused. For an instant, she watched him considering her words. The sharp line of his nostrils widened, then relaxed.

"I see," he answered, slowly now with the growing warmth of triumph. "You consider having a private drink with me running out on your husband."

Carol's defenses fell away beneath the soft laugh that followed in the wake of his death blow.

*You confuse me. You've always confused me. How can you know me so well and yet really know nothing about me at all?*

"I didn't mean that," she said, but the words remained inaudible in her throat.

And defensively she thought: Why not? Why should I go on defending a husband who isn't here? Jonny is interested in me. In his own perverse way, he cares. Why shouldn't I go with him? Just for a few minutes. For old times sake. As a friend. George won't miss me ... he doesn't really care.

He steered her from the house to his Lincoln, double parked as though it were waiting for them ... as though Jonny had expected to find her there.

A gust of wind lifted a sheet of newspaper and slid it from the sidewalk into the gutter. Yet she did not feel cold. Her skin felt wrapped in a protecting layer of anticipation.

Quietly, without protest now, she bent and slid down onto the low seat. From the tray on the dashboard, she lifted up one of the half dozen pairs of sunglasses and balanced it on the end of her finger.

"Still hiding?" she said.

He turned the key in the ignition as though the rich sound of the motor were answer enough. What've I got to hide from?" he said, as they slipped into the stream of erratic traffic.

"I don't know," Carol said, needing to keep on the attack. If she stopped asking questions, then he would start. And questions might lead to revelation. Then where would she be?

"No need to hide any more, baby," he said. "I've got it all, don't you see? Everything. Everything we used to talk about. I made it, kid. I really made it."

His voice seemed to crouch in thickets of pleasure.

"I suppose you have," she persisted. "If one can call what you do making it."

"Oh, I see what the gripe is," he laughed, scratching a match into flame on the sun visor. "My reputation. Now isn't it just like you to worry about a foolish thing like that?"

He paused to light the cigarette that she had taken from her purse.

"Yes," she said, inhaling deeply.

"Well, I'll tell you a little secret," he said, "if you want to know something. I sleep nights. I sleep sound and hearty on a belly that's eaten steaks, resting on the best mattress money can buy, in any hotel suite I want in the whole world."

"That may be," she said bitterly. "But how long will it last? Another year? Two? And then the police and headlines and what kind of bed will you sleep on in jail, my friend?"

A snort of derision punctuated her question ."Morbid little girl," he said. "Or just naïve—I don't know which. Anyway, your idea is neither realistic nor to the point. You seem to forget that a business the size of mine supports the law enforcement agencies. They can't *afford* to stop my operations."

"Big time," Carol said, unable to disguise the nastiness in her voice. "Big-time pimp."

Chico sighed. "If that's how you want to see it."

Carol dashed the half-smoked stub into a gleaming ashtray. "How else is there to see it? Don't forget I remember you when you were taking quarters as your share from the kids in high school. Has it changed any since then, Jonny Chico? Or just gotten larger?"

"Both of us could do a lot of remembering, if we wanted to," he said with a bland ease. "But I wouldn't choose to be as unpleasant as you're being. I mean, if I were going to remember things ...."

Carol knew what he meant and the fight drained out of her. But she didn't want to go back to those times of tenderness. Of their love-making with its spontaneous innocence. Their dreams together. Of what use to rehash the youthful joys that could never happen again?

Her breath made a circle of vapor on the window as she turned her face away to escape him. The city lights strung out along Park Avenue seemed to encourage her to remember the present. Whatever Jonny Chico was or did shouldn't concern her. He had no part in her life any more.

"Anyhow," his voice interrupted her thoughts, "you can always do me the courtesy of remembering that I do have another profession."

Oh yes, she remembered. And it was just this ludicrous pose as a health specialist that drove her furious. How many times had she tuned in to his radio program and listened with disgust to the seductive voice advising women about their intestinal tracts and the resilience of their bone marrow. And how many times had she passed a book store only to encounter his smiling, professional calmness on the dustjacket of his latest? Yes, one way or another, Jonny Chico owned the world of women. He had made them his own private circus.

"Where are we going?" she said dismally.

"Some place warm," he said. "Where we can sit down and stop fighting for a few minutes. Some place where we can relax together and enjoy whatever it is we always enjoyed together."

Carol's throat went dry with quick shame. There was no mistaking what he meant. She had been a virgin before Jonny. And he had shown her, taught her, developed the fine details of her enjoyment. The times they had spent together—the good times— were the times of honest physical pleasure, without a sense of guilt or inhibition.

"Take me back," she said desperately. She felt a surging need to fling herself out of the car.

"To the party?" he said. "Or backward in time?"

He was mocking her. The cruel streak that could whip her alive with anger and frustration.

"Jonny," she rasped, "this is now. I'm married to a man of dignity and prestige. You can't toss me around as though we were still kids."

"A man of prestige," he mimicked, turning a corner sharply so that the sunglasses skidded to the far end of the dash tray. "Not an old whoremaster like me."

"Jonny, please. You've got to understand. You can't have your way all the time. Other people have needs, feelings just as important as yours."

"And you want to go back to the party?"

"Yes."

"You're a damn liar."

Carol swallowed hard.

"I mean it, baby. If you were so goddamned impressed with that husband of yours, you wouldn't be out here in this car to begin with."

Beneath her purse, Carol clenched her fists, struggling for control. "A nice, civil drink, you said. For old times sake. I thought we could be adults together, Jonny. But I see I was all wrong about you. You're still the nasty little bastard I knew way back when."

"The lady forgets her manners," he said, calming. "The lady is beginning to let her past show."

The car sailed now through Central Park. Shivering trees whipped by, shaking their desolate limbs toward the black expanse above.

"Your influence. I always seem to drop down a peg when I'm with you."

Jonny reached for a dial and switched on the radio to slow music. "The secret of my charm," he said.

From the radio dial, his hand moved down lightly to her knee. Through the thin clinging material, she felt the caress of his touch. *You can't do this,* she thought. *I can't let you.*

Yet what could she say to him? Please don't?

"I don't want you touch me," she said at last. The simple statement surprised her.

"Don't you?"

"No."

"Why not?"

"The answer is obvious, I think. Do we have to go into details?"

But his hand did not move away. For a panicky moment, she thought it moved slightly upward toward her thigh. Just for spite.

He could do that. Take what he didn't really want, just for spite. For the vicious satisfaction of showing someone who was boss.

And then the hand lifted.

"All right," he said. "I won't touch you. Not until you ask me. Not until you beg me," his voice grew intense. "And that, my little Bittersweet, is a promise."

His pride cut through her. She knew what it meant. That he believed with all his heart that she wanted him. Desired him. Craved him. Her legs began to tremble. This was not the safety she had hoped for. Not at all. His words were not a challenge, but an act of faith.

"Then we'll have a very moral evening," Carol said because saying it seemed to be her last chance of making it come true.

Jonny didn't bother to answer.

She pressed her spine backward into the yielding seat and tried to steer her thoughts into safer channels. What could they talk about? What had they ever talked about?

Only one thing had really mattered.

A forbidden subject between them now. At least for her. Her body felt like a drunken thing lurching and swinging through a rising heat of sensation. And her head, with its sage thoughts, seemed very far away from it all.

"Why did you come to that party?" she said languidly.

"To find you."

"Seriously."

Jonny shrugged. "I always go where there are women."

Carol's thighs stiffened. Ask a direct question, get an honest answer.

They had come through the park and worked westward onto the Hudson River Drive. The music and the vague outline of Jersey blended to dull the edges of her sensibility. Why press the fight? Why not lean back, as they say, and enjoy it? She had gotten into this of her own free will. She had better adjust to accepting the consequences ... whatever they might be.

Everything had happened so quickly. She could hardly make sense of it. The practical, cool young matron that she had been this afternoon ... where had that part of her personality fled?

The woman who sat now within her skin she hardly recognized. Wanton…adventuress…without thought for tomorrow. For certainly tomorrow would bring disaster to her marriage. Even if nothing happened tonight.

And nothing must happen. She knew that Jonny could never love her. Not really. He might pretend, might even want to. But it was not in Jonny to love. Only to take, to possess. She could not do that to George. Her departure would be disgrace enough. Anything more….

The car sped northward out of the city limits. Small private homes slipped by, nestled snugly behind well groomed trees.

"Yes," he said, responding to her unspoken thought, "I bought a place up this way some years ago. Never had much of a chance to live in it till two years ago."

"What happened?" Carol said acidly. "Did you break a leg?"

"Nope. Only my blessed state of bachelorhood."

Carol's spine stiffened with anger. His casual words were like a slap.

He chuckled. "A little thing like marriage shouldn't bother a big girl like you."

Carol lapsed again into silence. Chico was right, after all. She didn't really care that he was married. The woman Jonny Chico married could mean very little to him. Jonny was not the marrying kind. She had no idea who the woman might be. But she knew instinctively that she would have money and a name that meant something in the world. For Jonny Chico would not let himself be tied down, except from greed, from a need for protection of some kind. Love he could get anywhere…without having to pay.

She felt the car beginning to slow and soon swing off the highway to climb a winding gravel path beneath the thick foliage of trees that blocked out the sky.

Finally, they pulled up in front of a rambling garage.

"All out," Chico said lightly and came around to open the door.

"Your wife must be quite the social butterfly," Carol said as a final dig.

But Chico did not answer.

She felt his arm against her back, guiding her along the low stone wall that led around to a backyard of well trimmed lawn. Pool lights shimmered in the water, making grotesque shadows of floating leaves that swayed in the wind. Beach chairs and lawn umbrellas lay scattered as though dropped here by a careless destiny.

"You need a caretaker," Carol said.

"Well, something anyway," he murmured, the wind carrying his words from her.

To Carol, the forlorn display of wealth seemed to be the story of Jonny's life. His dissatisfaction sprawled before her, obvious to anyone who took the trouble to see. It seemed strange that a man with such strong whims and careless way of living could have built himself an empire of lust behind the purple robes of respectability. Instinctively she felt that somewhere in his life there hung a weak brick or loomed a crack in the foundation. He couldn't have all the ends sewn up. Too careless, too inconsistent to be thorough. She looked up at the rugged, lonely face and wondered how long it could be before his downfall.

Silently she followed him over the pebbled walk to a brick ranch house that seemed to cling to a slope of land.

"Home sweet home," Jonny muttered. "Complete with coke machines."

As he rang the bell, Carol realized that she hadn't been thinking about his wife. Something in his manner implied that she must be away. Divorced or separated or even dead perhaps. Living with Jonny could kill more than one woman.

The musical chimes focused her attention for the sound of answering footsteps.

They waited a moment.

Then another.

Jonny looked at her and raised his shoulders in a casual shrug. "Nobody in," he said, as though they had come as guests to another's home.

"Well?"

"What night is this?"

"Sunday."

"It must be the boy's night off."

"Boy?"

"You wouldn't want me to keep women servants, would you?"

Carol smiled to herself. He always had to play games. Complicate matters to liven things up. Life itself was too easy, not enough of a challenge for Jonny Chico. He always needed more drama. An adventure waiting for him just over the hill.

And perhaps it was this that created the irresistible urge to be with him, to forget about her own world and be with him wherever they might be. Fight. Make love. Struggle through the continual tangles of his life. At least it was *living*.

He worked out the key slipped in behind the nameplate and opened the door.

"Go on," he said. "No one's going to bite."

Carol stepped into a lighted foyer that led off to various rooms all alive with light.

"Con Edison must love you," she said.

But when he didn't answer, she sensed again the acute loneliness that he worked so hard to hide. He couldn't come home to a dark house, just as he must always run around to parties, surround himself with admirers, acquaintances, even enemies. For company. Any kind of company.

"Well, anyhow," she said, filling in the rest of her thought aloud, "I do make an excellent baby sitter."

He was standing with his back to her, pouring drinks. She could see his arms pause for an instant in midair.

"The best," he said.

"What's the matter, couldn't get a date tonight?" she said, letting her body relax onto the oversized foam rubber chair. The bright reds and browns of the room did not seem his choice of color. She wondered if the wife he mentioned had purposely decorated the place in jarring colors.

He came around to lean over the back of the chair and handed her a glass. His fingertips paused along the inside of her arm.

"You like giving me a hard time," he said. "And I like making things easy for you. That's why we get along like cats and dogs."

"Cheers."

Quietly, she drank, needing the bracer to keep her chattering alive. She felt unreal and disorganized. In the center of a crazy dream that had suddenly come true.

Whatever she did tonight would be unbelievable. She had left her good sense, her experience, her self-preservation back at the party with George.

"The thing to do at this point," he said, "is to light a fire."

"What for?"

"I don't know," he laughed. "Just to be conventional. Fires seem to stir the sex drive."

"They only put mine out," Carol said.

Jonny's eyebrow went up. "In that case," he said, "we certainly won't ..."

Without finishing the sentence, his hand slid up the full length of her arm and cupped her breast.

She dared not protest. She could feel her own breath hard and shallow. No doubt he could feel her heart beating. She would only be a fool to tell him no. No ... when she wanted to lose herself.

"I hate you, Jonny Chico," she whispered and finished her drink.

"Yes, darling."

He managed somehow to keep his hand on her as he came around to the front of her chair and knelt to rest his chin on her lap.

"I like the smell of you," he said. "The human smell that comes through the perfume. My little Bittersweet. Never got tamed. Never got civilized. Sometimes at night I would think about you, baby, and wonder how any man could keep you quiet long enough to grow moss."

Carol dropped the empty glass onto the carpet. No use trying to pretend. The final touches of her false decency had dropped away. Jonny knew her every bit as well as she knew herself. And it was lovely to be naked like this. Naked in her soul for him to see and love and desire.

She stretched her arms toward him and spread her fingers through his hair. "Make love to me, Jonny," she said. "And stop all this talking."

She leaned forward to meet his mouth with her lips, then straightened a little till her breasts pressed against his face.

His arms pulled her forward and she slid off the chair. The tight gown strained and she felt a struggling desire to rip it from her body.

The carpet welcomed her, deep and warm, absorbing the sound of their weight together.

"I always loved you naked," he said.

His hands moved to unfasten the hooks that ran down the back of her dress.

The touch of him shivered her flesh into tiny flames of expectation. He unhooked the garters and followed the stocking tops down the line of her thigh with his tongue.

"Sonofabitch," she whispered.

They rolled together on the welcoming carpet. An odor of stale ashes from the fireplace singed sourly at her nostrils. Autumn, cold and spare and lean, threatened outside. Soon winter with sparse brittle trees. But now, now at this moment she could warm herself at the sudden flaring of warmth that had dropped into her destiny unbidden. She must hug this to her. Nurture the precious warmth within her own body.

The hard pressure of his mouth flung Carol back through the dark tunnel of fifteen years. Her blood pounded and coursed with the light fantastic fire of her responding.

His hard chest pressed and bruised her. Her mouth opened on a dry throat of pleasure.

"You're torturing me," she said against his shoulder. But the pain of her waiting was hard and bright as an exquisite gem.

Her limbs stretched as though to draw in the universe. The vessel of her craving yawned, yearning...yearning....

*Oh, let us not die.... Keep us alive within the circle of this love forever...keep us alive to share it....*

And then her body arched on the pyre of its own sacrifice.

# CHAPTER FOUR

NIGHT LINGERED at the windows.

She lay stretched at random, her cheek barely touching his naked shoulder. Years seemed to have gone by. Or centuries. But still the darkness hung outside, waiting patiently for her return. A twinge of restlessness prodded vaguely. She turned and moved her body in closer to him, needing the reassurance of his physical warmth.

His hand passed lightly over one naked breast.

"I'll light the fire now," he said, moving gently out from beneath her.

"Will it help?" she said.

Chico nodded. "Always does. Drives away the demons, you know. Night devils are afraid of flame."

He understood her and it comforted his restlessness. She sat up to let him go and began slowly rubbing her feet on the high nap of the carpet. Their empty glasses stood on the floor just out of reach and she eyed them thoughtfully.

"I've got to go back some time," she said.

His body crouched at the hearth arrangings bits of newspaper among the fresh logs. From a brass container he withdrew a long match and struck alive a wall of flame. The glow spilled over his shoulders, making shadows of bone and rib and muscle.

"Come here," he said.

She moved in closer to the sound of crackling twigs. The acrid tang caught and flung her far from thoughts of city, of people.

"We burned a helluva lot of food at those damned beach parties," he said with a private amusement in his voice.

Carol knew the memory and nodded. Somehow, their lovemaking tonight had recaptured those feelings of spontaneous vitality. Of life without selfconsciousness. Young animals eager and free in the world.

"Would you go back to those days if you could?" she asked.

"I don't know." He shrugged, putting an arm around her waist. "What for, anyway? The poverty? The snatching things on the run?"

Carol restrained herself from answering. For men, the goals were different. His values all had to do with success and power and pleasure. She couldn't expect him to desire the love, the mystic security that she needed. Only this could give her true nonchalance about petty things.

Despite their momentary closeness, they were really very far apart—as they had always been. And in a way it was no different from her relationship with George. She had loved them both, each in his own way. And George, perhaps, had loved her in return. But not Jonny. Jonny only wanted her, for as long as she could satisfy him. If she lost sight of that truth, it could destroy her.

"I'd better start getting dressed," she said.

"What for?"

His question seemed strangely honest. Carol smiled. He hadn't a single thought beyond the moment. No responsibilities lay heavy on him. No burdens of tomorrow clouded his dreaming.

"I envy you," she said, moving to free herself from his touch.

"For what?"

"Your life."

"Oh?" His voice lifted with delight. "And just a minute ago you were smearing it hard and heavy with all the dirt you could find."

Carol nodded. "I suppose that was my naïveté speaking. I really think it's wonderful how you can take what you want whenever you want and never be bothered."

"And who stops you from doing the same? There's no ban on it, you know."

Carol took his lighted cigarette and inhaled deeply. "That, my dear Jonny, is what makes you so delightful and me such a bore. Here I sit, cozy, more satisfied than I've been in years … and what am I thinking of?"

"I can't imagine."

"You're making fun of me."

"Why not, Carol, wife of eminent scientist? People like you go through life giving yourself hemorrhoids. Always trying to squeeze out another little piece of guilt. Well, enjoying the moment is as much a matter of self discipline as anything else. I mean, if I wanted to start worrying, there's a goldmine of troubles waiting for me."

"So you prefer to be blind to them."

"That's not it either." He turned around and laid his head on her belly.

The pressure of his skull sent a thrill of sensation down her thighs. Bristles of his fresh haircut tickled her skin. Carol braced her weight on stiff arms. What difference did it make after all, his way of looking at life? Or her own? They were here together. Sharing something surprisingly important. Their love-making seemed to have shifted all the little pieces of herself, rearranging the pattern into something fresh and vital.

"I wonder if I will ever see you again," she said, musing aloud to herself.

He turned his head to look up into her face. "Why shouldn't you?"

"Every reason in the world, my darling." She held her stomach tight, trying to fight off the need to touch him again.

"But you will …. And we will …. You know that."

She let his head slip lower. "You don't need to seduce me," she murmured.

Her stomach felt as though it were sliding downward in a circular vortex. Her body was slipping rapidly out of control.

Slowly, he turned over. She felt the bony ridges of his forehead press against her thigh.

*I won't think about tomorrow.*

With both hands, Carol reached and drew him up along herself, sliding him with liquid languor.

A sudden, violent patter, like sleet, hit a window.

His body stiffened.

She felt his thoughts fly from her.

The perspiration along her arms went cold.

They sat up.

She waited, her glance fixed on him. All the angles of his face hardened. His expression seemed chipped from granite.

"Fun's over," she said icily. "Curfew tolls."

She watched him get to his knees and drag his trousers off the arm of a chair.

"Come on," he said, ignoring the thrust. "I'll drive you back."

"Don't make it sound like such a favor," she said. "I could just as soon stay for the show."

Carol whirled from him and began collecting her stray clothes. The gown seemed limp and just a rag now in her hands. Where had the prestige, the mystery, the chic flown? How incredible the fleetingness of an illusion.

Despite her anger, Carol hurried. She would not dawdle just to irritate him. Or perhaps it was just a reflex that made her try to fit into his life.

Again the pebbles on the window.

"All right," Jonny said under his breath.

As Carol dressed, she wondered who he was running away from this time.

"Your wife?" she said.

"Don't be silly," he said. "I don't run from women. Only toward." He tucked his shirt tails in with hasty thrusts. "Or maybe Scrappy's being cute. He does that to me sometimes. When he sees the lights are out."

"Scrappy?" she said incredulously. "Don't tell me you still keep him around?"

Jonny shrugged without bothering to turn around. "Somebody had to give him a job."

And watching him, Carol realized that his manner was too casual.

He kept a body guard! And if Jonny Chico kept a body guard, there must be a reason. A solid, frightening reason.

And Carol knew, without understanding why, that somebody wanted Chico dead.

She felt the cold hand of dread close over her heart. And yet she could empathize with whoever his enemy might be. Chico had never stopped to think about anybody but himself. Ever. He took what he wanted and used anybody he had to.

But this time he had slipped. This time he had crossed the wrong man.

# CHAPTER FIVE

"LET'S MOVE."

He switched the houselights into a blaze of brightness. Then he grabbed her elbow and steered her across the room, out the side door, down the stone steps to the car.

A cold round moon stared from behind smoky gauze clouds whisking along on the high wind. The night had become shadows of silver and stirrings. He thrust her onto the cold leather seat. The engine fired too loudly in the stillness.

Carol sat stiff-lipped and huddled in close to herself. She would not speak now. Would not distract him. His gaze seemed to burn through the windshield as they raced down the driveway. No time now for flirtations. For pomading the atmosphere with artificial romance.

He had taken her and that was all. She might as well face it. Now, with the trimmings cut away, she saw herself clearly. Too clearly. The mannikin of her body stood naked for her eyes to see—handled, stained with fingermarks that did not belong. Her skin quivered now in all the intimate places where he had touched her.

And now that he'd had her, he could throw her back. Onto the junk heap. What difference did it make to him? Just another woman. Another body....

Like all the women at whom she'd sneered...like Tammy and the love-starved, pathetic creatures in his radio audience. She'd been no different, no less pathetic than the rest. And worse, she had known that it must be this way. Because Jonny was Jonny Because Jonny could only love with his body. She had known ... and had given herself.

Wretchedly, she turned to stare out the window. Tried to forget whom she sat beside.

But the scene hung before her imagination. She saw herself again, naked. Writhing with delight in his arms.

Her hand reached toward the mass of tangled hair. Her tongue ran across her lips, dry now without make-up. It had all happened so quickly. And now she could make no sense out of why she had done it or what she had gained.

"I'm sorry," he said, as they bumped from gravel onto the wide asphalt of the main highway.

"For what?" she said, trying again for the light tone that usually helped.

"Business before pleasure, and all that." His toe pressed on the gas pedal.

"Of course."

"Don't be so damned amiable."

"It's my nature, Jonny. Or don't you remember?"

Her bitter tone hung in the air. She could not forgive him. Could not forgive herself.

"I'll make it up to you, Carol, I promise."

"Make up what, dear? It seems to me everything happened that was supposed to. A little rushed toward the end perhaps. But what difference? We would have had to part sooner or later. Why quibble about a few minutes?"

She needed something to do. Something to rein back the rush of nerves threatening to choke her. She opened her purse and searched for comb and lipstick.

Her face in the compact mirror seemed washed away, as though rain had soaked her features and run off to fade. She steadied her elbow against her side and created a full red mouth.

"But you didn't tell me," she said with the old flair for nonchalance. "Why are we running?"

Imperceptibly, she tilted the mirror to observe Jonny's reaction. She saw a tendon in his back go taut—but only for an instant. The vise of control took over, holding his expression steady.

"You don't want to know the sordid details, my sweet."

"Don't I?"

"Well, you might. But it doesn't make good bedtime reading, believe me."

"As you wish, Jonny. I don't pry."

But she wanted to pry. Crazily, she felt an overwhelming surge to know all the details, to watch them mingle and separate, to see Jonny from every viewpoint. Try again to know him. Make the futile attempt to understand.

"And then again," he said, "if you know it all, you won't find me interesting any more."

Carol listened to the words and knew that he had struck home with utter clarity. If she could only dissect him and survey all the parts, then she stood a chance of shaking herself free. But this way, grazing by him in the dark, she would continue to be tantalized by the ever-present mystery.

"You're probably a very prosaic person, actually," she said. "I've always held the theory that there wasn't anything at all in those big black shadows you always fling around."

She heard him laugh and knew that what she had said was very funny in a way she couldn't possibly understand. The vexation of it threatened mightily. She didn't want to plunge into depression. Into the gloom of sensing that life was really passing her by. That she had had her chance with Jonny Chico and muffed.

"But why should I be thinking about you?" she said. "I have my own shadows."

She had said it to be airy. But the words brought back George. What would it do to him, seeing her like this?

"Carol has shadows?" Jonny said. "Bittersweet never worried about herself."

"The hallmark of a child," she said archly.

But she knew it was true and she yearned for her old capacity to shrug off complications.

"Jonny," she said gently, "Jonny, I don't want to change this fascinating topic but I've been watching that same pair of headlights in your fender mirror ever since we turned out of the driveway."

"Hard on the eyes, isn't it? I suggest, then, that you don't watch any longer." He took out a fresh package of cigarettes and gave them to her to open. "Now, what were we saying?"

"Jonny..."

She didn't want him to shield her. But how could she make any claims on him?

"Light two cigarettes this time, will you? I'd like a whole one for myself for once."

Obediently, she lit the cigarettes. But she couldn't tear her eyes away from the too-bright reflection. No matter how she stared she could not make out either car or driver.

She handed him a cigarette. "Jonny," she persisted, "are we living a grade B movie?"

"Meaning what?"

"I don't know what I mean. Only... that car isn't following us, is it?"

He glanced at her briefly, then into the rear view mirror. "Would you like to find out?"

A cold thrill wriggled along her sides. Things like this didn't happen. Not really. In the blink of an eyelash you nod your head to something and the next day find yourself written up in the center fold of some cheap newspaper. No, things like this were impossible. Especially for people married to other people like the staid, important George Trace.... *The body of Mrs. George Trace was found....*

She inhaled deeply on her cigarette and watched the tip glow in the darkness.

"Yes," she said, "let's do find out."

As her sentence ended, the car lurched forward. She stretched out her feet and crossed them at the ankles. Her toes felt numb and her fingertips burned. Her gaze remained fastened on the sideview mirror.

"Well?" Jonny said.

"Well what?"

"The lights are still there?"

"Uh huh."

"Not smaller?"

"No," she said bluntly. "Same size."

"Fine."

She felt the car leaning right as they tracked off from the center lane. The sparse traffic seemed to part and fall away as they sped on.

"You know," she said, "I've never been in the habit of noticing other cars. Bad luck, it always seemed to me. Like recognizing the possibility of an accident and focusing on it till the darn thing happens."

Her voice was a monotone. She felt like a witch conjuring up devils.

"Never mind the philosophy," Jonny said around the cigarette jutting from his lips. "I'm my own rabbit's foot. Been my own good luck for almost thirty years."

He sounded so sure of himself. So steady. Steady almost as the lights she watched.

"Hang on," he said. "We're cutting off now into a turn that the highway department built, I think, to separate the men from the boys."

How could he sound so young and full of fun about it? He made it a game. Didn't he understand that the person in the other car intended to kill him? Or didn't he care any more? If he were anyone but Jonny, he might even think he deserved it. What had he done this time? Whose woman had he stolen?

But her thoughts cut dead as the car veered wildly. A high squeal cut off all hearing. Her arm slammed against the door handle. The car tilted and skidded high on the top edge of a banked curve. The tray of sunglasses slid, bounced against the vent window and fell into her lap. A stench of burning rubber seeped into her nostrils.

They bounced off the highway and cut between trees into a grassed area that she knew could not be a road.

Simultaneously, he switched off the headlights.

Hardly breathing, she sat still, watching in the mirror. Something scuffled on the tree trunk beside the window and disappeared high up into the leaves.

Minutes they waited. Minutes that hung heavily on her chest.

Then, some twenty feet away on the road, a car jounced by. Its country beam swept through the silence.

It was several seconds before she dared to turn her head and follow the fan of light till it melted out of sight around another curve.

She watched him, unwilling to speak until he gave the signal. The touch of clean country air flushed over her skin, contrasting its peace with the floundering of her heart.

After a while, she could not tell how long, Jonny started the car again and they backed out slowly.

In a moment they had found the highway and continued in silence toward Manhattan.

Soon, he switched on the radio. The easy manner of his movements blended into his angled cheeks and widened the firmness of his lips.

"Well, I guess that answered your question," he said, turning for an instant to smile at her.

Carol nodded dumbly, too unsure of her voice to speak. Besides, how could she dare to ask him the millions of questions flooding into her mind?

Questions, Carol realized, that she would not be able to shrug off easily.

As she could not shrug off the remembered touch of Jonny's mouth on her body.

# CHAPTER SIX

THE PATTERN of city lights blinked Carol back to reality. The jarring dissonance of taxis, the bottleneck of cross-town traffic seemed to loosen the stretched fibers of her being. She had no idea what time it was.

"To Paterson's or your place?" Chico said.

Carol honestly didn't know. She couldn't imagine how George would react to the discovery of her absence. Whether he had gone home with his embarrassment or remained stubbornly in an effort to ignore such a catastrophic blow to his reputation.

"Paterson's," Carol said finally, hoping that George would have managed to inflate his ego sufficiently against her behavior.

Chico laughed. "You're quite a girl," he said.

Carol raised an eyebrow in question.

"...Still," he finished the sentence with emphasis on the compliment.

She didn't bother to answer him. No need to tell him that she couldn't care less about the smirking glances ready to greet her. Chico would laugh in her face if she told him that her only concern now was for George and what would be best for him. No, Chico had never needed anything from anyone. He could only sneer at George's attempts to endow the lab. Besides, how could she explain to herself the difference in her feeling for the two men? Chico was a disease. An itch she needed to scratch at. An irritant that centered her attention. An uncontrollable point of desire demanding relief.

And George, the husband to whom she had vowed her loyalty. To love, honor and obey... In one night, she had destroyed the pledge of seven years' duration.

"What time is it?" she said, needing an anchor to hook herself back into sensible living.

"Two-thirty."

They had been gone only three hours. In three hours she had changed her life more drastically than in all those seven years with George. *I don't really want to go back,* she thought. *I want us to go on riding through town and out the other side.*

Carol braced herself on a deep breath as he slowed the car in front of Paterson's house.

"Here we are," Chico said, swinging himself lightly out the door. "In case you hadn't noticed."

She let him escort her up the stairs. Pretend. Wear the mask. Stroll in with the manner of a lady. Hide the whore beneath the dress. Hide the anger and the boredom and the private set of barbed wire feelings not permissible to ladies.

The great room, as they entered it, seemed curtained with smoke and the rancid odor of stale olives. No crowds now. No artificial vitality enlivening voices. The scratching of an old record played somewhere the fluted sounds of a Caruso rendition. A few limp couples were draped over various chairs. The litter of cigarette butts, toothpicks and bits of food made an awkward design across the rug. No tray bearers. Only empty bottles everywhere.

"How times do change," Chico whispered. "Wonder where the old man is."

Anxiously, Carol scanned the room. No one seemed to notice them or care. They seemed to Carol like human debris.

*He's gone,* Carol thought. *He's home killing himself about it.*

Her knees began to tremble. All the bones in her seemed to dissolve. She moved to an empty chair and let herself fall into it. An icy film of dread began to gather along the insides of her arms. How would she face him? What could she say after these seven years ....

Dimly, she noticed Chico going from bottle to bottle draining the last drops into a glass.

He brought the half-full glass back to her.

"Go on," he said. "It'll help."

Gratefully, she swallowed the sweetish, burning liquid. "You'll have to take me home," she said and her voice trembled now without shame.

"Fine." He squatted beside her. "But not till you tell me you're all right."

The Caruso record began again, repeating itself unnoticed.

"It's so damned hot in here," she said, her voice harsh with the smoke.

"Wakes usually are," he said. He patted her hand.

She leaned back and closed her eyes, needing to block out the listless room of cast-offs. But her lids would not remain still. They seemed to jump up and down as though rigged to sparks of electric.

And as she sat like this, hovering between despair and hysteria, she saw George come bounding through the entrance.

She could hardly believe it. The ruddy, triumphant look on his face glowed in the dismal atmosphere. His shoulders seemed more erect than usual as he puffed out his chest in the familiar posture of accomplishment. She sat, hardly daring to think as he approached her.

From his lean height, George peered down at her, a crooked, happy smile deviling one side of his mouth.

"So here you are, darling," he said in a brisk yet apologetic tone.

Carol remained still. After seven years, she still could not tell when he was acting and when he was sincere.

George rubbed his palms together, then lowered his fists into his jacket pockets bulging them carelessly. He seemed to rock backward onto his heels.

"I've kept you waiting a long time," he said "Haven't I?" The apology increased, coloring his words now with a tinny ring. "Three hours. A long time to leave one's wife ... one's beautiful wife in the company of ..." his glance found Chico.

"... Yes, Jonny Chico," Chico said, standing up.

Carol watched George extend a hand and shake Chico's.

*What kind of insane farce ...*

"How do you do, Mr. Chico. But in your distinguished company, I'm sure Carol was well taken care of."

George turned back to Carol. His movements, all military, crisp and self-satisfied, froze her. Would he kill her when they got home? Or himself?

"Shall we be going, Carol? I'm sure I left you long enough."

Carol did not dare to glance at Chico. Puppet-like, she pushed herself up from the cushions.

"I'll get your wrap," George said.

She watched him stride across the room, his sleek hair gleaming, his shirt and cuffs still fresh.

She felt Chico lean his weight in close to her.

"He doesn't know," Chico said.

"Don't be ridiculous."

"But I'm sure of it."

"Impossible. He's just more of a gentleman than you realize." She spoke swiftly, certainly, not daring to believe Chico's words.

"No. Just more of a fool."

"Jonny." His name exploded from her lips, chastizing and angry.

"Okay," he said gently. "Bet you a bottle of beer." And he began to move away from her. "Phone you in the morning."

"Don't bother."

The force of Carol's anger flung her toward the door to meet George. Watching his overblown selfesteem made her stomach begin to churn in rebellion. How dare he be so pleased with himself! And yet ... perhaps it was an act. A calculated maneuver to save both their feelings of pride. She stared at George as he strode across the vestibule, her wrap swinging from his arm. Stared at him as though he were a stranger. Nothing in his manner betrayed him. She could find no clue to a lack of sincerity.

"Well, here we are, darling." He placed the fur on her shoulders and patted her briefly, distractedly. "You must be stiff with boredom."

Carol felt the familiar mask of casualness beginning to slip over her features. Her pounding heart seemed to be knocking vainly against the thick, closed doors of her chest.

"That's how it is sometimes," she murmured, wanting to shake him awake, needing to scream at him, fight with him, see blood. Anyone's. Even her own.

She let him lead her outside into the cold, gray air. One of the taxis from the line that Paterson kept in hire for the evening pulled up.

She waited till George had settled himself beside her and given the driver their address.

"Was it worth it?" she said, softly, probingly.

"Carol," he said, and put his hand over hers.

His skin felt warm for once. Warm and intimate. Almost human, she thought.

"It must have been a momentous evening for you," she said carefully.

George sighed and let himself slide down on the seat. "I can't begin to tell you." He seemed to be speaking to the heavens.

"Well, try," she said.

George grinned. "Try? How can I say it? You know what I did? I got his mother on my side, Carol. Can you imagine? The old dowager moneybags herself. It was one of those strange accidents of time and place," he said, his own voice furred over with wonder. "I was waiting for Paterson in the library. He said he would meet me there. And I thought that I might just as well go on into the kitchen for a cup of tea. You know, sobriety and sincerity to make friends and influence people."

"And in the kitchen you happened to run into the old dame," Carol said. George's knack for drawing things out was particularly irritating tonight.

"Approximately," he said.

"And you just casually happened to get into a conversation with her."

George nodded, smiling, flushed, bright-eyed.

Carol leaned against the cab door to survey him. "I don't know what you've got, George," she said. "But somehow, you never lose, do you?"

"Enthusiasm, that's all it is, Carol. Plain old enthusiasm draws 'em all in like a magnet."

In the close quarters of the cab, she could not escape from him. Nor from her own revulsion.

"Besides which," George continued, "the habit of winning procreates itself."

Carol huddled into her corner, listening to the self-interest that blinded George to her. Any other man would notice when his own wife was missing. Or when she had been through an ordeal. Surely, she must look disheveled in some way. Surely, if he cared at all, he would sense something—offer some concern.

Yes, any man but George.

And then again, how could she be sure ....

"I wish you luck," Carol said.

"I have all the luck I need," George smiled. "Now." He paused to smooth the suede gloves over his knuckles. "I have luck in the palm of my hand. Mrs. Josiah Paterson is my luck."

The taxi delivered them and George, in warm silence, opened the door to their apartment.

Carol stepped into the familiar home surroundings with a shock. A well of tears rose behind her calm eyes as she crossed the living room toward her own bedroom. How different she was from the person who had left. How different George was. It seemed that the two of them were swinging swiftly to opposite ends of the world. He on the brink of success. Herself on the brink of destruction.

# CHAPTER SEVEN

CAROL LOCKED the door of her bedroom.

If he tried to make love to her tonight, she would kill him.

Or herself.

She tore off her clothes and went to stand in a steaming spray of shower. Closing her eyes, she lifted her face to it.

*Wash Jonny off me,* she whispered prayerfully. *Please let me forget him.*

But even as she stood there praying to an unknown force, she was already thinking about tomorrow.

He would call. Yes, Jonny would keep in touch with her now. She had revealed to him her need and she could not let him go until the burning ache inside her died.

Her skin pink and hot from the shower, she climbed into the wide bed and stretched her tired legs to wait for oblivion. Yet she could not sleep so easily. In one evening her life had become complicated to the point of disaster. No longer was she the respected, protected Mrs. George Trace. No longer the safe and secure matron.

In one evening she had traded the dull security of her life with George for the excitement of loving Jonny Chico. She knew in her heart that she loved him, that she always had. Not the way she had loved George, quietly and steadily—but wildly, irrationally, responding to his blatant maleness with the driving intensity of her desire, needing desperately to be with him.

She sat up in the empty bed and stared across the dark room to the flashing light of the Empire State Building beckoning through the black sky. Would daytime never come? Her breasts hung heavy, twin weights from her chest. She flung herself onto her belly and pulled the pillow over her ears. She must do something. Something definite to free herself from the forces that had risen so unexpectedly.

But what could she do?

Tell George? Confess it all?

But if he didn't know, why ruin him now at the height of his career?

Then divorce him. Free them both from the sham of their life together. She had every reason now to divorce him—concrete, burning desire for another man.

Carol's mind began to whirl with alternating and mingling thoughts of George, of Jonny. They screamed in her ears as the first orange touches of dawn sifted through the skyline of buildings.

Sounds of Monday morning reached her. Her skin felt brittle and dried out, her brain weightless in space. She was never much good without sleep. The draining sensation of circles beneath her eyes pulled her face taut.

Carol glanced at the small clock. She would wait here until George had dressed and left for the lab. Difficult enough to face herself, without facing him too.

She waited and watched the fragile gold hands till they reached eight o'clock.

Then she leaned out of the bed and pulled open the door. Silence. The pervasive morning silence that told her he had already gone.

Now what?

*I'll get up and make breakfast and pack a few things. Even if I don't divorce him right away, I can't possibly live with him a day longer.*

She slid her feet into the pink slippers and curled her toes against the softness of rabbit fur lining. She needed something to claw at her, not softness.

From the closet, she took out a pair of stretch pants and slipped them over her nakedness. The elastic hugged her hips and clung between her thighs. Carol stared down at herself and realized that she looked like a tramp. The thought comforted her somehow. No more pretense. Let the truth show. Let things be out in the open from now on, where she could catch and deal with them.

Barefoot, she padded into the kitchen, aware of her breasts bouncing beneath the striped polo shirt that she had slipped over her head. No brassiere. Free, the way she liked her body. Free and ready for anything. Ready for ... Jonny.

As Carol scrambled eggs in the big frying pan, the telephone began to ring.

*He's anxious.*

She let the smile of satisfaction play full on her face, savoring her pleasure. She had given him a good run for his money last night. He couldn't wait for more.

Carol sauntered to the wall phone and lifted the receiver, letting it hang from her shoulder by the rubber grip. One hand held the pan of eggs, the other a fork.

"Hello," she said, spearing a flake of egg and lifting it slowly to her lips.

"Why, Carol Trace, of *all* women to surprise *poor* little me with her social prowess."

Tammy's voice needled through her expectancy. The egg went cold in her mouth. She set the pan down on a nearby cupboard and steadied the receiver with her hand.

"I was just having breakfast," she said helplessly.

"Up so early after *so* little sleep? You're a regular athlete, aren't you, darling?"

Carol felt the impulse to make a return thrust but she held herself rigidly in check. There was something in Tammy's manner that she couldn't quite trust. What did she want at this hour of the morning anyhow?

"All right, Tammy, out with it."

Carol wouldn't feel offended if she spoke straight from the shoulder?

No, Carol wouldn't mind.

Well, then, just between the two of them ... could it be possible ... would Carol be a good sweet little girl and introduce her to Jonny Chico, *privately?*

"But you met him last night, for heaven's sake. Why privately, Tammy?"

"Why privately?"

The disbelief in Tammy's voice startled Carol.

"Well, I simply *don't* have your *courage,* my dear. I mean, Marvin is weak minded and all that but I couldn't possibly thrust a thing like that in his face. Not *directly,* that is. You understand. I *know* you understand."

Carol slapped the phone into its cradle and stared unseeingly at the eggs cold and soggy.

If Tammy could be so blunt, then George must know, too. He wasn't in a vacuum, after all. Even if he had been with old dame Paterson all night, it must have trickled through to him. Somehow.

The phone again, jarring her screaming nerves.

Would it be Jonny this time? Or Tammy again? Or who else that had thought of a way to take advantage of her indiscretion?

But she couldn't let it ring unanswered.

Holding her breath, she lifted the phone again.

"... darling, *wait* ..."

Tammy's voice.

*Wait for what?* Carol thought. *For you to strangle me?*

"... You know how blunt I am sometimes. I didn't *mean* to hurt your feelings. *Really,* darling. I only hoped that you with your *big* heart would do selfish, silly little me this wonderful favor."

A pause.

"And if you did," Tammy's voice tilted up and down tantalizingly, "I could do *you* a tiny, tiny favor in return."

This time, Carol couldn't hang up. Something about Tammy's tone... "Such as?" she said.

"Such as helping *you* to keep *Riker* from telling *George*. Need I elaborate?"

Fists began to pound in Carol's stomach. Could it be true? Was it possible that George really had been spared... at least so far?

"Darling," Tammy persisted, "you don't have to answer me before breakfast. Why don't you have a little something to eat and then ring me back? We've always been *such* good friends."

"All right," Carol heard herself acquiescing.

After she hung up, Carol stood staring at the eggs, her thoughts far away from breakfast.

How easy to do Tammy her favor.

And by doing it, save George from the disaster that had not yet occurred.

Why not?

Such a little thing.

Riker. If Riker told him, he'd make it twice as slimy. Build dirty word pictures. Drag George all the way down. Down farther than he deserved.

Even if she didn't love him any more, she didn't have to be needlessly cruel.

And this could be her second chance. She could thrust Jonny from her now. Cleanse herself. Return to the fold. Be the respectable wife.

"But I don't want to be a respectable wife." She flung the words at the walls. "I want to live a little."

Wretchedly, Carol turned from herself, from the hungers of her flesh. From the strivings of stunted life within her. This might be her last chance with Jonny. How could she give him up?

With trembling hands she put water to boil, needing the stimulant of black coffee to settle her raging nerves. Everything was pressing down on her. Hard. And so immediately. If she only had a little time to think, to plan, to reason out what was best for all concerned.

But life didn't work that way. It didn't wait. It just happened. And if you got caught in the middle, then that was just tough.

She spooned a heaping pile of instant coffee into a mug and poured the bubbling water over it. Then three teaspoons of sugar. She craved sweetness. Energy. Her ribs made a sharp pain against her sides as though they were filing through her flesh.

She would have to whip herself into action. Force her muddled head to think.

Yet there seemed nothing to think about. Her head roared with the thunder of Tammy's subtle blackmail. On a sudden crest of movement, she dialed the girl's number.

Tammy answered instantly.

And when Tammy said, "Hello," Carol said. "Go to hell."

Then she banged the receiver back down again.

She could feel her blood beginning to boil through her veins. Her temples throbbed. In another few moments, she would be sobbing hysterically.

Leaving the coffee untouched, she stalked back into her bedroom. From a shelf high in the closet, she swung down an overnight case and bounced it open onto the bed.

What she needed now was action…fast, furious, unreasoned action.

Carelessly, she stuffed in blouses, underwear and her two best suits. This would last her at least till the end of the week. And beyond that, she didn't dare predict. If Jonny wanted her, he would help her. And if he didn't…

She shut off the whirl of her thoughts and concentrated on finishing the packing. It seemed to calm her somehow. She zippered the case closed and sat down beside it to light a cigarette and stare at the telephone. It would ring again any minute now.

And this time, she would welcome Jonny from the complete fullness of a free heart.

# CHAPTER EIGHT

THE TELEPHONE remained stubbornly silent.

Carol got up finally and walked around the bed. She noticed lint on the rug and stooped to pick up a bit of thread. In the quiet, she could hear the faint hum of the electric clock. But she stopped her eyes from seeking the time.

He had not, after all, said exactly when he would phone.

And then the doorbell. The chimes sing-songed through the room with a faintly mocking tone. A delivery boy, perhaps. Something from Gimbel's that she'd ordered and forgotten about. One of the petty details of everydayness. Sluggishly, she went to open the door.

"You," her voice rang with disbelief.

"And why not me?" Jonny leaned an elbow against the door-frame and grinned.

"Well … I—I didn't expect you, that's all."

"But, dear, you never do." With a hand on either of her arms, he moved Carol aside. "You don't mind if I come in?"

"Help yourself," she murmured.

"I got to thinking about you last night. Naturally."

Hardly listening to his words, Carol followed him through the foyer. Her gaze drank in the outline of him, the boyishness of his slim hips beneath the suede jacket. She wanted to fling herself at him and hang on. Draw from him the strength she could not find in herself.

"...So I thought I'd drop by for a minute," he continued. "Take a quick look-see at the dump you live in and the kind of life that's been keeping you in wraps all these years."

Carol let him talk without interrupting. She felt no need to answer. The morning's build-up of tension began to ebb, turning into golden droplets of vitality.

"Well, don't look too hard," she said at last.

"Oh?"

Slowly, she moved toward him across the room. She stood very close, leaning her breasts lightly against him.

"Kiss me," she said.

She unzipped his jacket and slipped her cold hands inside. His body warmth flowed through her. She lifted herself on tiptoe, reaching for his mouth with her own.

"Good morning, little sunshine," he whispered against her cheek.

Carol closed her eyes tight. The odor of his skin and its roughness twitched her nostrils. All of her seemed to be reaching up from her belly, straining toward him, striving to become one with him.

"You don't know how much I need you," she said hoarsely.

His hands grasped her waist and began massaging down along her hips. Eagerly, her tongue forced his mouth open. Her body became an all-consuming lava that needed to engulf him, roll hotly over him. Cold crevices of air from his clothing mingled with the searing need of her own desire. With a quick thrust, his hand reached down and cupped her.

"The bedroom," he said gruffly. "I want to have you in George's bed."

Her head swung dizzily. She didn't care if he wanted to on the stage of Carnegie Hall.

"Let me walk," she whispered, moving his hand away.

She led him into the bedroom where George slept.

The air smelled of lilac after-shave. In a brief, electric flash, Carol envisioned George's face. The steady, cocksure glint of his eyes.

And then Jonny grabbed her breasts and tumbled her onto the rumpled bed.

She hit the mattress and bounced. Jonny flopped down beside her and rolled his weight to her. The edge of his jacket zipper cut her lip. She felt a quick sting. Then it was buried in numbness as his mouth caught hers. A corner of quilt tangled between her legs. The odor of George's sleep rose around her ghostlike.

"Take me away," Carol groaned. "Oh, please."

She felt his insistent tugging at her slacks and lifted her hips while he pulled the elastic material down over them.

"You sonofabitch," he said to her sudden revealed nakedness. He said it with laughter.

Carol understood his tone. The incredulity, as though he thought she'd been expecting him all morning. Maybe ... maybe, in some mysterious way, she had been expecting him. Expecting Jonny was her way of hope. Loving him, her way of life. He brought her alive and she wanted to live. He wanted her ... and she wanted to be wanted. She understood that now. Understood it with joyous revelation. She could do anything. Anything wonderful or dirty. She would drag herself through anything to be near him. Even sleep with him in George's bed.

Because Jonny held the secret of her life.

Carol braced her feet on the bed and lifted her hips. Her body arched in offering.

"I love you, Jonny ... Can't stop loving you ..."

"Baby."

His mouth and his hands and his knees probed her, touching, exploring. Slowly. She felt the exquisite, delicious touch that goaded her on higher. Her hands found her breasts and lifted them toward him.

"Take me." The words were mere mumbles of passion.

And George's bed squeeked and squealed beneath her. Her legs and arms entwined with Jonny's. She held him. For life and forever, she would reach toward this one man who could turn on the lights of her craving.

She rolled with him sideways over the pillows. Her head hung over the side and vaguely she could feel a rush of blood as it thumped through the bridge of her nose. Her eyes stared and saw a chest of drawers upside down. She felt him slipping a pillow beneath her back. Her jaw hung open. The skin over her belly stretched taut and she clung to the back of his head to keep herself from falling.

Sudden pain washed through her insides. But she didn't want to come back up on the bed. She wanted to hang like this, with the world whirling madly upside down. Somehow, everything made better sense this way.

She felt the weight of him sliding toward her. Sliding as he moved, thrusting them both farther and farther off the bed.

"Jonny..."

They fell off onto the carpet. A low laugh escaped her lips as they rolled half beneath the bed.

The insides of her knees pressed him, held him.

Her nails caught the edge of his flesh and dug... and dug, till at last, all of her relaxed away like the petals of a flower opening to the sun.

They stayed for a while in silence.

Finally, Carol opened her eyes. Jonny was looking at her, his own expression calm, faintly amused.

"Our private fallout shelter," he said, nodding up at the naked bedsprings above their heads.

"Uh huh," she sighed and closed her eyes again. Weakly, she ran the tip of her tongue along his forehead, enjoying the salt taste of his skin.

"It's a lovely morning," she said, pulling herself back to wakefulness.

"Great."

"So what have you learned about …" Carol paused, wondering why she had to keep right on thinking about George. The disgrace to him knifed through her. She began to wriggle out from beneath the bed.

"Hey," Jonny began, still clinging to one breast.

"This is silly," she said abruptly, not wanting him to see the distress choking up through her pleasure. "Come into my room, for heaven's sake. I need to get dressed."

Carol stretched for his hand and tugged him along with her back to her own room.

"So?" Jonny said, letting himself flop into an overstuffed chair.

"I'll be ready in half a sec," she said with forced brightness.

Jonny stretched his legs and surveyed the spread of his toes. "For what, exactly?" he said.

"To go," she said, pulling open a dresser drawer.

"But you don't like my place," he said. "It's too dismal."

Carol sat down at the mirror and began the careful job of her make-up. Something prickled her about Jonny's tone. She couldn't quite grasp what it was.

"Besides," he continued, "there are people lurking all over. We'd never have any privacy."

"Like last night," she said dully.

"Yes."

His answer was too flat, too definite. It took the steam out of her.

"But you can stay at my office, if you want." He took a cigarette from the porcelain box on a side table. "There's a suite of rooms behind it. You'll be quite comfortable."

Sharply, she glanced at his reflection in the mirror. "Are you sure?" she said softly.

"Of course, stupid. You think I want you staying here with this gink that's burying you before your time?"

To herself, Carol sighed with relief. She returned to the job of her lipstick and finished it swiftly.

"Beside," he said, "I see you're all packed."

"Your own fault."

"For kidnaping you last night?"

"Yes."

"A fortunate fault," he said, blowing smoke toward the ceiling.

"Maybe for both of us, Jonny."

"How?"

Carol touched a drop of perfume to her earlobes. "Maybe I can keep you so busy that you won't have time to stir up the kind of trouble that gets people chasing after you at two o'clock in the morning." She heard the edge of worry fluttering unashamed in her tone.

"Oh, blow off," Jonny said, laughing.

But his manner of dismissal did not shake her. There were some things that a woman had to do, after all. And one of them was protect the man she loved from his own foolishness. But she couldn't say this to Jonny. He would only laugh.

"We'll talk about it some other time," Carol said. "Now, go put your pants on."

While he dressed, Carol took a last survey of the apartment that had been her home.

She ought to run out. Forget about everything. A word to George through their lawyer would make things clear enough. So what difference could it make if the sugar were back in the cupboard or left sitting out on the table?

Yet the force of habit, magnetlike, drew her from room to room. Her glance swept swiftly over all the little things that had been her existence and were so no more. The old upright in the music room, closed and waiting for New Year's Eve when they sang *Auld Lang Syne*. The canary cage on a shelf of the bookcase still waiting for George to buy the bird he had promised her but somehow never remembered to get. Yes, that's how it had been, her life with him. Always waiting. Waiting for pleasures that never arrived. Waiting for companionship. Waiting for ... for all the things that never happened and would never happen.

Quickly, she bent to the rackful of old newspapers stacked for the cleaning woman to remove. She straightened them and settled George's batch of scientific annuals lying beneath them.

On the memo pad in the kitchen she scribbled a note that said nothing really, she thought. But then again, George would not realize this.

She folded the paper and stood it on the sideboard in the foyer where George always dropped his hat.

Peering down through the layout of rooms, so hollow and still, made a small twinge of nerves come alive in her throat.

"Jonny?"

"Yeah."

She held onto the doorframe as she watched him coming toward her, his shirt collar open and the jacket collar up, one hand jammed into a trousers pocket, stance and step springy as though he were walking on new grass. She saw that he carried her suitcase, swinging it rhythmically in step.

He reached her and slowed down and tilted her chin up toward him. "Give me the key," he said.

Carol found the key in her purse and handed it over.

He set it down on the table beside her note.

"Okay, honey," he whispered, "Let's go."

And Carol slammed the door shut tight behind them, needing to hear it bang in her ears to make the moment quite certain.

# CHAPTER NINE

THE MORNING sun burned brightly into her eyes. The doorman tipped his hat good morning. Carol's feet felt attached to jellylike ankles. She stumbled down the street after Chico. The taste of autumn crackled in the tempo of traffic. An odor of burning leaves mixed with the smell of exhaust fumes.

"You want to walk awhile?" Jonny said, staring down at her.

She looked up at him without replying. In the daylight, he seemed not quite so hard or cruel.

"You know," she said, "sometimes I believe you're for real."

A grin brought hard lines into either side of his straight mouth. "Don't press your luck," he said.

Carol raised an eyebrow in question.

"I mean," he continued, "like the vampire bat, you've got to catch me at the right times." He grabbed her arm and hauled her through traffic to the Central Park side of the street.

Carol didn't answer. He had a way of making fun of himself, of others, of anything. You had to be on your toes to catch him serious. Or maybe it was true. Like the vampire bat and all. Only at night had she seen that other side of Jonny Chico. The man walking beside her now, touching her protectively, helping her, humoring her through a bad time...this man was not the bastard people whispered about. Carol let herself relax into a more optimistic frame of mind. No, she wouldn't press her luck. She would take Jonny at face value, any way he offered himself. And so far he had been very good to her.

"Where is your office?" she said, thinking to make harmless conversation.

"Half a dozen blocks from here." He nodded at her with glowing eyes. "That's right, baby. I've been only half a dozen blocks away for almost five years now." He grinned. "Ever since I came out of retirement."

Carol reached for his cigarette. "It would have been so easy," she mused. "I could have saved us both all this time."

"Forget it," Jonny said abruptly.

He didn't like to look backward, she knew. Always ahead for the next incident, the next excitement. The next bit of trouble he could stir up.

They strolled in silence beneath the trees on Fifth Avenue, crunching leaves as they walked, smiling at babies and old women. Incredibly to Carol, the world seemed all tidy. Nobody and nothing had fallen out of place. The brisk, clear morning was drifting calmly along—everyone engaged in prescribed occupations.

But she didn't dare think that her days ahead would feel so natural and normal as this interlude. Heaven only knew what awaited her when they arrived at Jonny's office.

They crossed Fifty-ninth Street, moving downtown past the lineup of horsedrawn carriages.

"Around the corner," Jonny said, steering her past store windows and into the revolving door of an ornate entranceway.

The elevator took them up seventeen floors.

Carol leaned back against one polished wall and thought how strange they must look to everyone dressed in correct suits and ties. Jonny the oddball. Jonny the nonchalant nut. Without selfconsciousness, he stood out in any crowd—a true figure of a man. How had she ever been attracted to George, when she had known Jonny's love? Whatever else he might be, Jonny Chico was a man who knew what he wanted and got it. Nobody had ever pushed him around. He had never crawled on his knees to anybody, the way George did all the time. Jonny Chico was top guy all the way.

The strange and delightful thrill of possession sailed through her as she watched him. As though by giving of herself to him, she had become a part of that virile life she found so attractive.

Reviewing it, she couldn't blame Tammy and all the others for trying to get close to him. Tammy, whose husband was the man with the big red ears. And the others... None of them had married men who could compete with Jonny Chico. Not the way women really cared about. Poor Tammy...

The recollection of Tammy's phone call sent a smile of satisfaction through her bones. Indeed, what would Tammy think now? Or could she ever be honest enough to sit back and be content to turn a mild shade of green?

"Seventeen..."

The doors slid open, interrupting her daydream. They stepped out into a plush, blue-carpeted vestibule with leather chairs and sofas. On the wood-paneled walls hung photographs of world famous people, autographed to Jonny Chico.

"Quite the glamour set-up," Carol said.

"Part of the game," Jonny grinned, moving ahead of her to push open a pair of huge swinging doors.

The clacking of typewriters punctured the air. Faces of pert secretaries tilted up to blossom good-morning smiles. The surface friendliness seemed formal enough. Yet Carol felt an intimacy just beneath the surface. An easiness between Jonny and these women that she found hard to overlook.

They passed down a long corridor through the sweet odor of bouquets set here and there on shelves. All of them red roses. The heavy scent of the flowers overlaid business with pleasure, Carol thought. Or was it romance....

Silly.

Her tense nerves could play mean tricks. But she wouldn't give in to them. And why ask questions anyhow? Anything

Jonny didn't want her to know about his life, she would never find out anyway.

And if he trusted her, loved her, then he would tell her everything. In time.

Carol followed him past room after closed room. "Isn't there another way to get through?" she said, her irritation needing some harmless outlet.

"Sure. But I thought you'd get a kick out of the grand tour. Chico Operations in operation, so to speak. Or doesn't it strike your fancy?"

"Not just this moment, thank you."

"Well, grin and bear it, honey. Just another few yards."

She could grin and bear anything. Just so long as it took her far away from the past and closer to Jonny. But this was not the place to be obvious about her feelings. She could tell by his manner, his sauntering gait, that he appreciated that she kept a slight distance between them.

"Here goes," Jonny said at last, pressing a buzzer.

They waited a moment and then two doors slid open to a circular staircase.

"What more?" Carol said.

"This is the end, I promise."

"You should have told me to wear hiking boots."

"Very funny," he said. "No, not up, sweet, down."

And she followed after him down the narrow metal stairs. Carol took a deep breath, but knew better than to comment. This office apartment of his was obviously nothing more than a bulletproof hideaway. Involuntarily, her thoughts snapped back to Scrappy's pebbles against the window and the pursuing automobile.

She paused in the semi-gloom while Jonny pressed another bell.

And then the heavy door swung open to a smiling face atop a tiny, twisted body.

At sight of Carol, the egg-shaped bald head began to bob and the wide, squashed nose seemed to spread across the whole face as it broke into animated smiles.

"You remember Bittersweet, don't you, Scrappy?"

"Of course he does," Carol said, bending down to embrace the man whose head shook even harder now with enthusiasm.

Scrappy's adam's apple bobbed up and down in voiceless greeting. Then he hopped back into the room, beckoning with both gnarled hands.

"He's telling you you should have come sooner," Jonny said. "But she's here now, Scrappy, and I want you to take good care of her."

In response, Scrappy began clapping his hands. Then he hobbled off to a sideboard and brought out a bottle of wine and some glasses.

"You'll burn a hole in yourself one of these days," Chico said, "drinking that stuff."

Carol took a half glassful of the almost pure alcohol that Scrappy drank. She could barely get down a mouthful. While she struggled with it, he bowed her over to a satin-covered chair. The only one among all the black leather furniture.

"Go ahead," Jonny said. "Sit down and kick your shoes off. We're all old friends."

There was no denying this, Carol thought, as a glow of warmth spread through her—partly from the liquor, partly from the three of them gathered together again. She could remember back when Scrappy had played chickie for them after school hours. A trusted friend and bodyguard. Though he looked harmless enough, Carol knew the extent of his temper and the prowess of that malformed body when his temper was aroused. If Jonny did indeed need a watchdog, she felt satisfied and secure that he had chosen to keep Scrappy around.

"Here's to old times and new ones," Carol said, closing her eyes and trying the liquor again. She felt somehow right in this weird hideaway. As though all the past, respectable days with George were a sham scraped off her now. In a wild moment, she had accepted the fleeting chance to start life over again with Jonny. And whatever happened would be her natural destiny. Without regrets, without remorse.

"Scrappy'll help you get settled," Jonny said, draining his glass. "I've got a show tonight and all the hassle that goes with it."

"Fine," Carol said, needing to be agreeable.

Like a well oiled machine, he slid up from his chair and moved toward the door. "See you back here later."

*When? Why can't I go too?* Carol stifled the questions behind a light nod.

She heard the door slap closed behind Jonny. He was going, only heaven knew where. Perhaps to other women of the countless number he kept on tap. Carol slid her elbows along the satin material, feeling the sensual pull of its wave. This would be her chair. To sit in .... To wait in.

"Scrappy," she said to the little gnome of a man she loved like a brother, "let's get drunk."

# CHAPTER TEN

S LOW SWIRLS of dizziness circled round her. The haze padded all sound, softening the large silence that pulsed in her
ears. A line of sweat trickled down her spine. There were no
windows to peer through, to steady herself by turning in on the
time of day.

A hiccough cricketed through her chest. She blinked heavy
eyelids and managed to smile at the little man born in the shape
of something she might be looking at through water.

*Don't you ever get lonesome? Don't you ever want someone to
make love to you?*

Drunken thought, she realized. Questions not to be voiced.

"He's been gone a long time, hasn't he?" she said.

Scrappy hopped out of his chair and held up three fingers
close to her.

"Is that all?" she said. "It feels like days."

Scrappy lifted his shoulders in agreement.

"Or maybe it's because I don't know what to think when he's
gone. You might not believe it, Scrappy, but I've learned how to
worry. You poo-poo it, eh? Well, that's because you know what's
going on. I only get to see the surface, after all. And grapevines
can be pretty nasty."

Scrappy shook his head and patted her knee for consolation.

"If I could walk," Carol said, "I'd ask you to show me through
this mausoleum he calls an apartment. Couldn't there even be
one window?"

Scrappy tugged at the leg of her slacks.

"All right, I'll try," she said. "But the room is spinning."

Carol pushed herself out of the chair and lurched after him as he hobbled ahead through a narrow hallway. Through doors that stood ajar, she saw packing boxes piled high and wooden crates. Odd pieces of furniture placed without reason. An old television set, two yellowing refrigerators.

But the final door opened into a pleasant studio arrangement with pink papered walls and a high slanting skylight that illuminated the clean white bureaus, divan and tweedy rug.

Scrappy pointed a finger from the room to her.

"Mine?" She watched Scrappy nod. "Or just any old whore's room, tell me the truth."

Scrappy's lips went white. She could see the tautness transform his face to a concrete mask.

"I want to know about it," she said, dragging him to the divan and sitting him down beside her. "I've got to know so I can help him. You understand that, don't you? People chasing after him in the middle of the night. I've got to know who and why. But I don't dare ask him, Scrappy. He only laughs at me."

She could sense the little man's blood pounding harder through him.

"You don't have to be afraid of ratting on him. I'm not the cops or his wife or anybody that can do him any damage. God help me, I love him, Scrappy."

Scrappy put his finger over her lips to stop the unnecessary demonstration of her feelings.

"All right, I won't try to force you," she said at last. "Maybe in your own time, you'll come to trust me a little. The way you used to do."

She watched the sorrowful cast film over his bulging eyes. He wanted to tell her, Carol realized. But her presence had happened too suddenly, her request had been too pressured.

"And maybe you're perfectly right not to tell me while I'm fozzled," she smiled. "I'll take a shower and unpack my things and go to bed like a good little girl." She bounced on the springs. "That'll sober me up and I won't be in the way till Jonny gets back."

Scrappy looked at her with a reproachful twist to his flabby lips.

"Well, I'm sure you have better things to do than to look after me," she coaxed.

Then his whole face lit with a sudden idea to please her. And Carol, seeing this, felt somehow reassured that she was not taking Scrappy's attention away from where Jonny might need him.

While she crossed her legs under her on the bed, he rushed over to a set of double cabinet doors set into the wall and pulled them open. With a quick movement, he flicked on a television set.

"You mean, sit here and watch his show?" She could barely keep the hurt tone from her voice.

Scrappy shook his head a violent no and moved his fingers like spider legs through the air.

"We can go see it?" Carol said.

Scrappy nodded.

With a burst of appreciation, Carol flung her arms around the hunched shoulders and planted a resounding kiss on his scrubby cheek. "I knew you wouldn't desert me," she whispered.

Then she pushed him from the room.

With light hope, Carol began to unpack her few possessions. In time, Scrappy would tell her everything she needed to know. She would win back his confidence and maybe together they could help Jonny straighten out the threatening tangles in his life.

Restless and hoping for some clue to the truth, some odd scrap of information, Carol searched all the empty drawers. She peered behind the shower curtains and poked in the medicine cabinet of the small bathroom. Everything seemed so neat. As though even the fingerprints had been washed away. How strange that all signs of the previous inhabitant had been erased so completely. Almost as though she were searching for a ghost, Carol thought and shuddered with a sudden chill.

But she forced all such contemplation from her mind. It would not do to get morbid. Worry only put wrinkles where she didn't need them. And she would need every scrap of appeal she could muster. After all, why kid herself about the competition? It was all there—alive and itching to get its claws into Jonny.

Carol pulled off her slacks and began to massage the flesh over her thighs and up along her hips, working the remnants of tension from her body. Her routine days, through which she had walked as though blindfolded, had become hectic scatterings of minutes around her. She could no longer predict what lay ahead. But one thing was certain. She would need all her nerve and reflexes to cope with the way of life Jonny had to offer.

Drawing on the depths of her discipline, Carol forced herself to lie down on the firm mattress. Carefully, attentively, she stretched the network of muscles that relaxed one after the other, down through her fingertips. Rushes of cold passed along the sides of her naked breasts. Memory of Jonny's lips touched her in odd places and she smiled dreamily....

At last, she sat up again and proceeded about the business of dressing for the evening. The skylight above was growing gradually darker as the slow curtain of night descended. Jonny was a night time man. He always came alive after dark to burn with that steady, bright flame irresistible to women.

Carol snapped on the two torch lights and set her flat heeled shoes on the floor of the deep closet. As she bent down, the narrow strip of wall to wall carpeting curled away from the corners. Slovenly, Carol thought. The rest of the room so precise and this bit of rug so badly laid. It seemed out of place.

On impulse, she grabbed one corner of the rug and pulled it away.

What she saw nearly catapulted her backward. She sat down with a violent flop. Her mouth went dry as she stared at the wood scrubbed so hard into deep gashes—scrubbed desperately, it seemed. Yet not deeply enough to remove entirely the splotches of dark stains. Carol held her breath and tried to swallow the revulsion. She could tell blood when she saw it.

"Scrappy." Her lips formed the name but her voice would not come out clear on the first try. "Scrappy," she called again hoarsely.

The door flew open and Scrappy lolled in the doorway, his head tilted inquiringly.

Wordlessly, Carol pointed.

He rushed forward and banged the closet door shut.

*"What is it?"* her wide eyes said to him.

He turned his back to her and raised his fists toward the ceiling. Then, as though she had unleashed something terrible inside him, he picked up an old telephone book and began tearing it through.

Carol leaped to him and spun the little man around to face her. She saw the whites of his eyes bloodshot now with rage. The odor of liquor on his breath reeked rancidly.

"You must tell me," she said, shaking him. "Was there a murder in this room? Was there?"

Scrappy emitted a huge sigh as though the balloon of rage in his soul had suddenly burst.

"Then what?" Carol persisted as he shook his head no. "What does it mean?"

For answer, Scrappy tapped her wrist watch.

Carol pressed her lips together and let her grasp on him loosen. He had gained control of himself once more. And she knew he would tell her nothing.

"All right," she said. "I'll be ready to go in a minute."

And then she realized, as he realized, that she was standing there clad only in bra and panties.

In the wake of his riveted stare, she ran to the bathroom and slammed the door shut between them.

She waited, listening, until finally she heard his uneven step leave the room. Then cautiously, she came out and slipped quickly into one of the two suits she had been about to hang into the closet.

# CHAPTER ELEVEN

THE AUDIENCE sat hushed in their warm, plush seats. A pencil beam of light ushered Carol down the slanting aisle.

"When can we go backstage?" she whispered to Scrappy as he helped her to settle in.

His cupping motion told her: later.

Well, later was better then never, Carol thought, glancing about at all the women eagerly waiting to see her Jonny.

Then her gaze roved to the stage—the oversized show boxes of Vitafoods and the oversized, bosomy broads glowing with Vitafoods health. For one green jealous instant, Carol shook with the realization that Jonny must have sampled everything on that stage. But everything. An urge of nausea arrowed to her stomach. She swallowed hard, trying to force a lid down on her uncontrollable feelings. Prickles of cold dotted her cheeks and lips. She clung to the velvet arm rests.

But it was no use.

"Scrappy, excuse me, will you?"

Before he could answer, she got up and began pushing her way along the poking knees. The end of the row seemed miles away.

At last she reached the back of the auditorium. She glanced white and inquiringly at a stationed usher. He pointed and she raced off through the lobby and down some steps.

A babble of female voices high with hilarity trickled out around the edges of the rickety, pinewood door. Then, moving among them like an anchor sinking to depths, she heard Jonny.

Carol stopped. The wave of desperation in her stomach seemed to freeze quite still. She sauntered up to the door and stood there, listening.

Though she could hear the tones clearly, she could not make out the words. The blur of merriment teased at her. She could just imagine Jonny, his arms around the shoulders of two of the semi-naked women, kibitzing. Enjoying himself as though . . .

As though . . . what?

Had she no claims on him?

Was she just another piece of meat hovering in limbo above him?

The nausea turned to icicles of anger.

Carol strode forward and flung the door open before her.

"Why, Mrs. George Trace, of all people. Come on in."

The voice that welcomed her was not Jonny's. Carol's head swiveled to where a crowd of girls, stage-dressed in thigh length skirts, moved aside revealing the seated, smiling figure of Tom Paterson. And as he greeted her, Carol saw that he made no effort to remove his hand from the buttocks of one of the girls.

She felt her tongue go dry with embarrassment.

Two six-foot brunettes in a corner giggled. They stood close together, their swollen breasts touching.

"We're having a little party," Tom continued. "Too bad George couldn't join us." His fingers crept a little lower down on the black-stockinged leg.

Instinctively, Carol's glance sought help from Jonny. Yet the moment their eyes met, she knew she had made a mistake.

"So you two really are old friends," Tom said with a hearty, knowing drawl. He smiled at Chico. "I'm surprised you never mentioned it, Jon. You're not usually demure about your conquests."

Chico's scowl darkened. "It's not like that."

Paterson smiled again. "Perhaps," he said. "But you have a way of captivating women I . . . admire."

Carol glanced from one to the other of them curiously, hearing the subtle undertone of conflict, yet unable to pin it down. Chico had hurt everyone who knew him in some way. What had he done to Tom?

Jonny's eyelids closed and opened slowly. His eyes shown black and bright with his contempt as though reaching for her, wanting to strangle her for her stupidity in coming here.

"You might as well join the crowd," Jonny said with a twist to his words that she had never heard before.

A hand grazed over Carol's shoulder. She saw gold-lacquered, long nailed fingers linger on her flesh. "Hello, hon," a female voice said with breath that smelled of thick raspberry lipstick. "I'm Mitzy."

Carol throttled her desire to pull away from the touch. No one had invited her in, so she must take whatever happened. *Can't you see, Jonny? I'm part of everything you do, everything you are. I'll drag through the lowest, filthiest gutters for you. Just love me.*

"Save it," Jonny said to Mitzy. "We've got a show to do. You'll get mussed."

"Oh, pooh," breathed Mitzy. And in a movement of impotent rebellion, she turned around and flicked her almost naked behind in Jonny's direction.

"Beautiful," Paterson chuckled. "I must take that home to Mother."

"Stuffed and mounted?" Jonny said, snapping back into good humor.

Carol knew she must fit in with the festivities. "Looks stuffed enough to me," she said, trying to make the words delectable.

There was a second of silence during which everyone in the tiny room stared at her, as though trying to assess this newcomer.

Then Jonny burst out laughing. The ring of his voice relaxed the stiffness.

Carol felt her eyelids blinking rapidly with gratefulness. He had forgiven her. He accepted her. She could be one of the inner circle now.

She watched him elbow his way through the girls to her. "Everyone get dressed," he said to the room in general. Then he poured something from a silver pitcher and handed it to her.

"Cheers and all that rot," he said to her.

She lifted the thick orangy liquid and tasted.

"Carrot juice?" her voice squealed.

"And why the hell not?" he said over the confusion of voices and movements as the girls began pinning high, pink plumes into their hair.

"And it's not even spiked," Tom added, coming toward them. Affectionately, he draped an arm over Carol's shoulder. "But don't be frightened," his voice reached intimately toward her earlobe. "The vitamin A will make you see in the dark."

"With her eyes closed," Jonny added.

A large red bulb over the door began to flash.

"We'll leave you to your business," Tom said, suddenly businesslike. "And pick you up after the show."

To her surprise, Carol felt Tom beginning to tug her toward the door. Again she glanced quickly at Jonny for her cue. Imperceptibly, he nodded.

Because Jonny wanted her to, Carol permitted Tom to lead her outside.

As they crossed the lobby together, she could feel herself coming apart both inside and out. Somehow, her clothes didn't seem to be fitting properly. As though strange hands had molested her, twisted the seams of her stockings and her self respect. She longed to submerge herself in a hot tub of something and come out miraculously newborn. To start all over again and remain alert so that situations didn't rush on ahead of her, leaving her breathless and always trying to catch up.

"Come along," Tom said. "We'll go to a nice, cozy bar and get that carrot juice taste out of your mouth."

"Oh, I don't mind health foods," Carol replied hastily. "It's just the time of day, you see. I think vitamins belong with sunlight, not evening."

She had to fool along with him, find out just what was expected of her. After all, Moneybags was Jonny's sponsor. And maybe he was behind Jonny in some other way, too. Renting women from him for some fantastic price. Or heaven only knew what.

"You sound like George," he said, steering her through the congestion of traffic and across the street. "A very precise but imaginative man, your husband."

Carol couldn't tell whether or not he was mocking her. His high, white hair blew slightly in the wind, emphasizing the tanned ears and neck. He seemed so robust, so sure of himself. An attractive man with all the money he could want, he should have had no trouble finding women by himself. It seemed out of place that he seemed to be using Jonny's services in that way. There must be something else—some factor she had no way of knowing—that kept Tom Paterson interested in Chico.

"George is a very sweet man," Carol said. "In many ways."

She felt Tom appraising her. But she felt confident that he could not see through her mask. And her statement about George was true. If Tom wanted to trap her for his own reasons, he would have to try something other than prying into her relationship with George. If, indeed, he cared about George at all. Somehow, she didn't think so.

Tom walked briskly and on the narrow points of her high heels, Carol had to work to keep up with him. Obviously, he was not wandering aimlessly to kill an hour till Jonny's show ended. Remembering Jonny's silent directive that she go with him, she wondered what both of them had in mind for her.

But whatever it could be, she would do it gladly. Do it for Jonny. Prove herself no prude. Make herself useful to Jonny. Establish again the trust he once had in her. Yes, she would have to devote much time, much strength and all her ingenuity to the task of rebuilding the closeness that she had destroyed many years ago.

"You know, your husband is going to be a famous man some day."

Carol agreed without saying anything.

"Perhaps the Nobel Prize or something," Tom persisted. "With his brains and application, all he needs is the equipment. That makes all the difference, you know. Enough staff, the proper machinery or whatever it is that scientists use. Yes, indeed, Carol. Money... money properly applied could make that man."

Paterson's words stabbed at her like gunfire. He was aiming at her purposely and with a malicious hint of something. And instinctively she felt that it was Chico he was after in some way, not she. But why?

"I have complete faith in George's ultimate success," Carol said and felt her words blowing away on the wind.

"So have we all," Paterson concluded with a cryptic drop to his tone.

Abruptly, he veered her around a corner. The street, lined with closed stores, seemed almost like a dark alley compared with the Avenue. Toward the center of the block a lone sign hung, its pink neon letters sputtering.

"Here we are," Paterson said as they came up to the narrow, single doored entrance.

The dingy exterior opened into a long, polished bar with glasses and display bottles on immaculate glass shelves. A scattering of people, all of them well dressed, lounged at the counter or more intimately at the small round tables set well spaced at the back of the room. Carved coconut shells and ebony statues of island gods stood on small wall shelves. The blending of modern sophistication with tribal witchcraft created an undertone of passion that Carol could not quite define. She knew only that somehow this décor touched her where it hurt, in the places she must keep hidden from the world.

Ahead of her, Tom led the way back along the tables and toward a corner of the room lit by a deep yellow bulb high above. Carol could feel him heading straight for the woman sitting behind a stem glass half filled with a rose colored liquid. She wore a hat shaped down from the style of a man's fedora. Its brim shadowed the face beneath. Only the tense posture could Carol really make out. The woman's body seemed somehow quite noticeable beneath its draping of black woolen coat. Her face, almost hidden in the high fur of a fox collar, appeared open and direct. Without seeing the woman at all clearly, Carol felt she could sketch an intimate picture of her. And she could almost sense what was coming next.

"Have you been waiting long?" Tom said to the woman.

She leaned back against the chair and moved the glass slightly with her fingertips. "Not very," she said easily. "Besides, I'm accustomed to waiting for you, my dear. And I forget the time."

Although the woman looked directly at Paterson as she spoke, Carol knew that she herself was the object of close scrutiny. She stood quietly, letting it happen, aware that the woman obviously liked what she saw.

"I had an unexpected piece of good fortune," Paterson said, holding out a chair for Carol.

"I see you brought it along," the woman smiled at Carol, directly, openly.

Paterson took one Spanish peanut from a bowl on the white tablecloth. "This is Carol Trace," he said with explosive mildness. "George's wife."

"Oh, you know my husband?" Carol burst, suddenly unsure.

The woman smiled and her head tilted sideways. The yellow light shone on her fragile skin, outlining a soft youthfulness that concealed her true age.

"Why yes, of course," she said and her voice lilted with pleasure. "We met and became fast friends just the other night."

"Mother is very generous with her friendships," Tom said, rolling the nut along the cloth.

Mother? Carol worked hard to conceal her disbelief. Even in this dim lighting, she could see that the woman was younger than Paterson.

"Yes, Mother," the woman said, echoing Carol's thoughts. "Not biologically. Strictly marital."

"Mother," Tom explained, "was my father's second wife." He tossed a lock of hair backward with a quick motion of his head. "Am I not the most fortunate of children?"

Carol nodded. Watching him, she knew instinctively that Tom Paterson was in love with this woman he called Mother. Madly … and without response from the woman. Behind her easy grace, she began to feel suspended out of time and space again. She could understand Tom's feelings. She had often felt that kind of mute, strangling frustration loving Jonny. Wanting him desperately and knowing that he, in turn, wanted someone else. It had always been like that with Jonny, even in the beginning. Never had he been completely hers. And she understood that it was this elusiveness, as much as her deep physical attraction to him, that had kept her bound to Chico all these years.

And it was no different with Tom. Wanting this woman and forever denied, he would die for her if need be. Or kill.

"We were just talking about George," Tom said and motioned for a waiter.

"Then we needn't continue," the woman laughed. "I'm sure you covered the topic quite thoroughly."

On someone else's lips, the sentence would have been a slight to George. Yet on hers, it seemed an act of grace. As though she were releasing Carol from hidden chains.

"Tom is an artist at minor blackmail," the woman said lightly, looking to him for a cigarette as he brought out a flat leather container. "He no doubt prepared you with the routine of do-as-I-tell-you-or your-husband-goes-right-down-the-drain."

"Mother!"

"Now, now, relax, sweet. I don't think we have to play checkers with Carol Trace. I know you meant well but obviously, she's not a whore for my bed."

Carol felt her skin go cold and white.

"You don't mind a little directness, do you, dear?" The woman smiled straight at her. "A friend of Jonny Chico never minds directness." The smile tightened. "It's the way Jonny does things. Especially with women."

The words struck home. Without needing to be told, Carol knew that this woman had known Jonny, as women always did, too well. Had known him and would never forget him.

"No … not at all," Carol sputtered. "In fact, I'm grateful."

"Yes, of course you are. And you are wondering what to call me, aren't you, since you can't very well call me Mother."

A waiter's red sleeved arm set down three stemmed glasses. Carol stared at the drink before her, wondering whether she dare try to lift it with the trembling fingers she held tightly clasped in her lap.

"My name is Garril Royce Paterson," she continued smoothly. Laying the cigarette into a clean wiped tray, she leaned slightly forward. The black coat fell away somewhat, revealing a white silk blouse sheer enough to suggest an outline of her slip. The mold of her breasts gave a nicely rounded curve to the material as though it were being held up by the muscles and tendons of her own suppleness. "The few friends I have call me Garry," she concluded.

Carol heard the voice fuzzily beyond her own thoughts. A flurry of questions spun loudly in her ears. What time was it? What was Jonny doing right this moment? What had really happened between George and this woman in the Paterson kitchen the night of the party?

What would it feel like to reach over and touch that clean, clean clinging blouse?

Clamping her teeth together, she concentrated on getting the glass to her lips.

"Now that you've settled everything so quickly," Tom said with half bitterness, "I might just as well be going home."

"If you wish," Garril said. And leaning a forearm on the back of her chair she waited, watching him expectantly. "I don't see you moving," she prodded after a moment.

"You mean that?" Tom said.

"If your feelings are hurt, I see no reason for you to stay."

"But..."

"Come along, Thomas, the evening has no room for hurt little boys."

It sickened Carol, listening to the scene between them. Garril treating him like a child and Tom responding with the injured pride of a man. Vaguely she wondered if Garril realized the intensity of Tom's feelings toward her. Surely the woman must know that he was in love with her. And knowing it, why did she deliberately ignore it and feed his frustration? If she had any feeling for him at all, she must realize that she dare not push even Tom too far.

Abruptly Tom's chair scraped backward. "I know when I'm not wanted."

As he moved briskly out of the bar, Carol wanted to call after him. But a strange presentiment stopped the words.

"Let him go," Garril said. "He needs a good night's sleep anyway."

Carol let the breath out of her in a sigh. She felt not quite so sure now of what might happen next.

"Despite this unfortunate beginning," Garril said to her, "I hope to make the evening worthwhile. For both of us."

Carol finished her drink and felt it mixing with the potent stuff Scrappy had given her earlier. "I'm sorry, Mrs. Paterson," she said. "Since I can't give you … whatever it was I was supposed to give you, I'll just go back to the theater." She caught the flicker of interest in the woman's eyes. "I'm expected," she added hastily.

"You love him very much, don't you?" Garril said, her tone a statement rather than a question. "Jonny, that is."

There was no point in being evasive. Nor did she wish to keep it a secret. The more people who knew she and Jonny were together, the better she liked it.

"I could shout it from a mountain," Carol said quietly.

Garril smiled, her fine mouth twitched upward at the corners in a subtle expression of intimate pleasure. "You are, my dear," she said.

"I've got to get back," Carol repeated and began to stand up.

"Certainly," Garril said, lighting another cigarette and making no effort to move. "And when you see him, tell Jonny that Garry sends her regards."

As Carol made her way toward the door, the small, twisted figure of Scrappy burst in. On his contorted face she read the concern and anxiety that her disappearance must have caused. No doubt he had searched for her and run into Paterson, who, in turn, must have told him where to find her.

But Carol felt too tired, too confused to make the effort of apologies. He confronted her, staring hard, his neck veins bulging and throbbing.

"Well, I don't need a bodyguard," Carol said angrily. "So don't start picking on me."

Yet through the redness of his fury, Carol could see that he wanted to tell her something. His limbs seemed to shake with the frustration of needing to express his thought. In final desperation, he grabbed her wrist and pulled her back to Garril's table. There he plunked her down on the chair and stood before her, arms on hips, conveying that she must not go away.

"Hello, Scrappy," Garril said. "Long time no see."

Scrappy ignored her.

"He doesn't like me," Garril said gently.

"Then why does he want me to stay here?" Because Scrappy could not talk to her in words, Carol felt herself reaching toward Garril for the explanations she needed.

While she sat, Scrappy took a stub of pencil from his shirt pocket and scribbled on a square of cocktail napkin: *Stay with lady tonight.*

Then, before she could protest, he turned and hurried out, jouncing grotesquely so that even the blasé clientele of Benje's Bar turned to stare.

"So," Garril inquired softly, "what do you intend to do now?"

# CHAPTER TWELVE

"I AM a tramp. I am one of the world's worst tramps off the street, but nobody believes me."

Carol's voice boomed and echoed inside her own head. She gestured wildly with both arms and bumped into the ornate lamps in Garril's bedroom.

"Undress me," she commanded from where she fell now, sprawled on the bedspread. "The price is right and I don't fight."

"Heavens," Garril said, sipping a cup of mulled cider at her boudoir table. "I hope you don't get drunk like this in front of strangers."

Carol flung herself over onto her face and mumbled into the pillow. Her breath felt hot and putrid, reeking in her own nostrils. Dimly she knew where she was and why. Painfully, she knew that Jonny had sent her out on a mission and that she was failing miserably. Clarity floated in sporadic blobs across her brain.

"All right," Garril said, coming toward her. "I'll undress you and you'll go to sleep like a good little girl."

Carol lay still, watching her. Without the imposing hat and the dark overclothes, Garril seemed even softer and younger than Carol had supposed. Auburn hair fluffed about the pale skin, emphasizing the deep eyes that seemed to change color with the changing reflections. As she moved a hand toward Carol's belt, an emerald bracelet slipped down the fragile wrist. Carol thought how cool the hand seemed, how good it would feel on her steaming forehead.

"I'm not as drunk as you think," Carol said.

Garril sat down on the edge of the mattress. She smiled without answering, while the cool, calm fingers reached upward to undo the row of pearl buttons on Carol's blouse.

"You're very good to me," Carol said softly and with more control. "I don't know why."

Their glances met for an instant.

"Because," Garril said, "you're in love with Jonny Chico. Anyone in love with Jonny Chico needs someone to be good to her."

As her blouse slipped down her shoulders, Carol listened to Garril's words repeating in her ears. She stared away to the small fireplace sizzling with a steady glow of embers. The room was beginning to come into focus more clearly, as though Garril's statement had shaken her back to sobriety. She had been right about Garril, then. Garril, who seemed to prefer women, had fallen prey to Jonny Chico, just as Carol herself had done. Had wanted him, had loved him.

"You know a great deal about him, don't you?" Carol said. "And perhaps I don't know anything about him at all...any more."

The dregs of alcohol in her stomach seemed to be bringing on a wave of despair.

"He's a difficult person to understand," Garril said. "He does strange things."

Carol's intuitions sprang alive. She sensed in the woman's manner an even deeper knowledge than she had expected. Or had wanted to believe. She had not let herself think that others knew Jonny even better than she did herself. Perhaps had meant more to him. But Garril's love for Jonny did not mean that she would be willing to help Carol. More likely, the contrary.

"What are you drinking?" Carol said, knowing that she could best get at Garril's knowledge through an indirect route.

"Cider. Want some?"

"It wouldn't sit," Carol smiled. "But if you have some coffee ..."

"Easily arranged."

Carol remained on the bed, her clothes half off, brassière showing through the opened blouse, her skirt zipper opened and stockinged feet crossed now at the ankles. But she continued to undress herself while the woman put a kettle of water to boil on a crossbar over the fire.

"Jonny's been getting me women for quite some time now," Garril said, her back curving as she bent down with the kettle. "I suppose you gathered as much."

"You don't seem to be the type, somehow," Carol mused. "To mix pleasure with ..."

"Money?" Garril laughed softly and spooned coffee into a Chemex.

"And if sex is a matter of business with you," Carol plunged on, "why won't I do?"

She had her skirt off now. She lay with her knees slightly parted, slowly unhooking the snaps of a white satin belt.

Garril poured the water carefully and watched it begin to settle down through the grounds. "Don't be so darned crass," she said mildly. "It isn't becoming."

"You sound like a kid," Carol said, wanting to shake the woman out of her self-possession. "A snot-nosed kid on his first trip to a whorehouse."

"Well, of course," Garril said, arranging cups on a tray, "if you insist ..."

Her tone of mockery stabbed Carol. She felt defeated at every turn.

"Look, it's simple," Carol blurted. "I've got a job to do and you're not letting me do it. Jonny sent me to you for a reason. How am I supposed to go back and say I wasn't good enough for you?"

"Then why tell him?"

Carol stared at her, puzzled.

"I don't pay for it piecemeal, after all," Garril continued, still unshakably calm. "But rather on a yearly basis. So you see there's nothing lost."

Chagrin barbed through Carol's stomach. If she couldn't seduce the woman, she couldn't hope to draw out the confidences about Jonny for which she yearned.

"Besides," Garril continued, "I would be thinking of George."

"In that case," Carol said, her temper stiffening in the joints of her elbows as she sat up, "I might as well leave."

"Now come along," Garril said. "You remember Scrappy's instructions, don't you? Obviously, you have no other place to go tonight. So just cuddle up under the quilt and forget about everything until morning."

At Garril's words, Carol felt a small finger of fear begin to tickle along the back of her neck. She hadn't realized till this moment that Jonny wanted her out of the way for some reason. Something was going to happen tonight that she wasn't supposed to see. She bounded from the bed.

Pulling her clothes together, she dashed for the door and ran barefoot down the carpeted stairs. Hall lights threw shadows so that she stumbled over mistaken corners and edges of things. In the darkness, she jiggled the knob of the street door, then searched with floundering hands for the lock.

"I'm sorry," Garril's voice called from the top of the stairs. "But you can't get out unless I buzz the door open from up here. Which I am not about to do."

"Why?" Carol shouted up at her. "What have I done to you?"

Her question echoed unanswered through the dark rooms.

Again she turned, unable to believe the ultimate truth of Garril's words. She clung to the doorknob and shook it with every drop of her ebbing strength.

Now she could feel herself beginning to tremble. A mixture of fear and desperation stirred hotly in the cauldron of her belly.

"Come back upstairs," Garril urged. "It's cozier here. And we can talk."

There seemed nothing else to do. Reluctantly, Carol dragged herself back up the steps. It seemed a long, futile climb.

"So," she said dully as she faced Garril once more, "the game was on me this time."

Suddenly she saw Jonny's tactics, cold and certain. He had wanted her out of the way tonight. And he had made certain of it by sending her to Garril, who loved and would help him. Was Jonny still in love with Garril?

"All right," Carol said, knowing that she would get out of this house tonight if it killed her. "I give up."

"That's sensible," Garril said. "Now we can return to the coffee. I'm sure it's ready."

Wordlessly, Carol followed her back to the bedroom. She sat down on the carpet beside the fireplace and stared into the dull red glow.

"We'll throw another log on," Garril said, "if you'd like."

Carol took her mug of black coffee and waited silently, sipping at the welcome stimulant while the flames began to lick upward at the fresh wood. Opposite her Garril too sat on the carpet, cross-legged in a pair of checked slacks.

"It could be pleasant," Carol said, "if we were friendlier."

"That's what I've been trying to tell you."

"I'll just have to forget that you're my jailer for the night," Carol said with a fresh lilt to her voice. Slowly, she began to stretch out on the carpet. "Mind if I put my head in your lap?"

"Not at all."

As the back of Carol's head touched Garril's thigh, she felt a flicker of nerve go up the woman's leg. She lay like this for a while, watching the bright flames draw upward and nurturing herself with the first seeds of encouragement. Despite Garril's overwhelming calm, the woman did have a human weakness. So there was hope.

"I feel so far away from everything," Carol said dreamily.

"Enjoy it."

Carol tilted her head back to look up at the woman's throat. "I'd like to." She touched Garril's forearm. The woman's arm tensed at her touch. The bracelet jingled almost inaudibly.

"Sometimes I don't love Jonny at all," Carol said. "Sometimes I hate him." She caught Garril's wrist with the palm of her hand. "Like now."

"The other side of the coin," Garril said quietly. "Love and hate."

Carol sensed that the woman had stopped resisting her. Since the door incident, a certain understanding had grown between them. She knew that Garril felt free now to respond with her body as before she had felt pressed to deny it. And she could almost hear an echo of loneliness resounding softly inside Garril. Money had helped her to solve nothing.

Pulling herself in closer, Carol raised herself up against the woman, letting their arms and their bellies touch lightly.

"We can both of us relax now, can't we?" Carol whispered.

For answer, Garril placed her palms on either side of Carol's face. She tilted her head upward toward her own.

"You have such young … such worried eyes," Garril said.

And then their lips met.

Carol had never kissed a woman before. The soft, yielding lips, the smoothness of face, the delicate scent of perfume aroused a strange thrill in her. Curiously, she pressed her body closer. What would flesh against flesh feel like? How would she respond to the touch of breasts against her own?

Their bodies lowered gradually to the carpet. Behind her, the crackling fire threw out a blossom of heat, enveloping her. Secretly, Carol's fingers crept up along the woman's side.

"Easy, baby," Garril muttered. "It's been a long time."

But Carol pressed only harder, thrusting herself to the woman, pinning her down. She felt Garril's reserve giving way before her like an opening flower. And instinctively, Carol knew what to do to help it along.

A windowpane rattled somewhere behind a curtain.

"It must be cold outside," Garril said, laughing in a gutteral voice. The spreading heat made a glowing orange of her skin. A fruit to be squeezed and sucked dry, Carol thought as her mind whirled in a brew of anger and grim lust. Despite herself, butterflies rose fluttering in the pit of her stomach. Her hands clawed for Garril's clothing.

"I need to see you naked," she said. "All of you."

Garril lifted her hips, helping now, as Carol pulled down the tight slacks. And then the nylon panties slithered away, revealing the roundness of hips, the firm thighs quivering with expectation. While Carol watched, she opened her own brassière and lifted it away. She cupped her hands beneath her breasts.

Carol rocked back on her knees. Her tongue felt thick and hot. Her eyelids burned with the strain of staring. She had never experienced this oddly vacant desire throbbing through her chest. Her fingers wanted to move, to probe, to know, yet they remained suddenly stiff and she pressed her knuckles into the carpet. A fencing of barbed wire seemed to be flung up between her body and Garril's.

"Frightened, baby?" Garril said. She made no move toward Carol but undulated her thighs slowly as though massaging herself with the thought of what would eventually take place.

In answer, Carol forced herself to lean forward. She lay down on her side and propped her weight on an elbow. "Should I be?" she said with a blasé tilt of her chin to hide the pounding of her heart.

"Yes," Garril muttered. "If you had any sense, you wouldn't take all this so lightly. You wouldn't try to write it off as a business venture. I know what's going on in your head. Lots of others have had such smart ideas. But believe me, they don't work. One doesn't get out of this kind of thing alive."

Carol leaned in closer. She rested her mouth against Garril's hip. "You're so very moral," she said against the warm flesh.

She had to keep the act going. Pretend she wasn't scared out of her wits. Talking only made her more nervous. She began to pull herself up along Garril's body, hoping to capture her once and for all.

But Garril sat up quickly to meet her. And Carol found herself suddenly in the woman's full embrace. She could feel the soft, well formed breasts sliding along her body, moving as Garril moved, almost as though with a special desire all their own.

Carol felt herself falling. Her thoughts stuttered, then faded out of focus. She knew only the sensations of her flesh, as the eager, pliable lips searched out intense excitement. Feathers seemed to flit through her. Bits of flame exploded and sizzled out. She came alive in splutters of growing desire.

Garril rested her gently down to the carpet. She stared with dry eyes at the gray-green ceiling that seemed to be floating like some ancient ocean above. As she gave of herself, she did not dare to look, to see with her own eyes the strange, tantalizing things happening to her body. Yet she recognized the different parts of Garril as they touched her.

Her body seemed to hum now, fueled by the heat of her desire. Her spine, her hips went into action, moving with an oiled smoothness. She squinted her eyes tight shut and reached to embrace the object of her need.

A sound issued from her own lips and a name.

Then the name faded and the obscenities came.

Carol said the words slowly, luxuriating in their sounds. Seeing pictures of the things she named. Seeing and tasting and smelling it all.

Yet she seemed to hover on the edge.

And then it happened ... happened, as she knew it must.

Gradually, Carol opened her eyes and brought Garril into focus.

"Well," Garril said, leaning back against the wall of the fireplace and lighting a cigarette with an overlong match. "What's the verdict?"

Despite herself, Carol felt a blush descending her forehead to suffuse her cheeks.

"We're not through," she said, stuttering yet with conviction.

Garril smiled to herself around the cigarette as she inhaled. "What do you mean?"

"I mean," Carol straightened her knees, "it was kind of … one way …"

"So?"

"So that leaves something to be desired."

Garril handed her the cigarette. "I like your delicate way of saying things."

Carol's arms felt heavy, her thighs wide and flabby with satiation. She had no interest in conversation. Forcing herself over to Garril, she took the woman in her arms.

"Let me," she pleaded.

Garril put her hands on either shoulder and tried to push her off.

"But I want to," Carol insisted. "I … must."

The urgency in her voice expanded between them.

"Really now," Garril laughed.

"Really," Carol pleaded.

She heard Garril release a long breath.

"Then put out that cigarette," she grunted.

Carol flipped the stub into the fireplace, then arched the woman close. She knew what to do and how to. She must use every method she'd ever heard of, tire Garril, drain her till she fell asleep.

For only then could she escape from the house.

Carol's lips parted and began their probing journey along the hot flesh waiting for her. The tip of her tongue savored the warm taste of salt and her nostrils were filled with the intimate odor of that special perspiration created by acts of love. She must give all of herself now. Rise with a terrific strength and draw the very spirit from Garril's body.

Suddenly, as she hunched over the body lifting itself toward her, Carol froze.

She saw herself hovering like a vampire, ready to suck blood. Her buttocks went icy cold and the chill spread upward along her spine. A lump of hard flesh seemed to rise in her throat.

*I can't,* she screamed inside herself. *Can't… Can't…*

And her hands, moving beyond her control, reached out for one of the ornate lamps.

Blindly, she crashed it down on Garril's skull.

# CHAPTER THIRTEEN

N UMBLY, CAROL got to her feet. The room glowed iridescent colors. Her eyeballs felt dry and cracked. Automatically, she flung herself into piece after piece of clothing until she was dressed. At the periphery of her vision, she saw one naked foot. Garril lay sprawled and silent.

She knew that she could not get out the front door.

What about the windows?

Opening one, she peered out and down into a back alley. A two-flight drop.

She hastened from the room and ran down the stairs, her trembling legs moving more swiftly than she could control. All of her seemed snapped into a vitality free from her brain's desire or direction.

On the ground floor she fled from room to room till she found a window opening onto the back courtyard. Then she climbed up onto a table and let herself drop the five feet onto cement. A sharp pain twisted in her ankle. But she kept running.

Out on the street, she came to a halt beneath a street light. Her breath felt like a thousand knives in her ribs. *What now? ... What now?* her mind screamed. She began running toward the wide Avenue, moving mothlike toward the pleasure, the reassurance of light.

But as she neared the corner, she stopped before a blue convertible. Vaguely, she recognized it. Garril's car? Had Garril driven her home in it? She peered in and saw that the keys still hung in the ignition. Of course. This would be Garril's nonchalance.

Carol let herself in and started the engine.

A shiver of dread ran through her as she sat in Garril's seat. But she needed to find Jonny now. Needed more desperately than ever to be with him.

She raced the engine and shot off into traffic.

Too late to find him at the studio.

Would he be at the house?

Or at the office?

Where?

The car nosed forward, moving almost of its own free will toward the highway. He had taken her to the house. Perhaps he took most of his women there. She would try it first anyway.

And expect to find ...

Her mind went blank. She could only feel. A nameless dread rolled greasily on her tongue. But she had to know. She had to find Jonny and know what he didn't want her to see.

It had been worth it to her, taking another woman's life.

Panic moved her hand to the radio buttons and she switched on a station of rock 'n roll, letting it blare through her skull. She pressed down on the accelerator. The speedometer needle began to move like the second hand of a clock.

Instinctively, she felt her way back to the right exit and careened off toward darkness and dirt roads. The radio blasted her presence, leading the way.

As she pulled up the driveway, her swollen lids narrowed to focus on the low, rambling house that lay flat and flooded with light beyond the shimmering pool.

She stopped as close as possible to the house, then leaped out and ran for it, hoping to make the front door before Scrappy could warn him.

The door gave to her pressure.

Seated on the couch, very sedate, very trim, and pale as death, sat Jonny. Opposite him, his legs dangling from a wing chair, Scrappy. And between them, straddling a straight backed kitchen chair with a glass of something bubbling in one hand and a small cigar in the other, sat a woman that Carol had never seen before.

The woman puffed a heavy cloud of smoke in front of her. Her bleached white hair hung in straggles to the low cut jersey blouse that hung out over a silver lamé skirt. She began tapping her feet and Carol saw that her sheer stockings led down to a pair of torn blue sneakers.

Her face emerged from the cloud of smoke. "Hi, honey," she said, waving the cigar. Her blue eyes glinted above deep, dark circles. She wore no makeup except pencilled eyebrows that seemed to stretch around her temples toward her ears.

Carol paused. The woman was a stranger to her, certainly, yet she recognized her from somewhere. A certain reminiscent fragility seemed to shine through the disheveled and wild incongruity of her appearance.

"You've had a short evening," Jonny said.

The acid in his voice cut through her. But she knew she could not explain, could not ask any of the questions puzzling her. Could not, above all, tell him what she had done.

Scrappy hopped off the chair. He ran over and bobbed before her like a buoy on a stormy sea. Whatever it was he wanted to communicate, Carol could not make it out. She saw it there, intense in his face, pouring blood beneath the surface of his puffed skin.

"Who's the doll, you bastard?" the woman said to Jonny. "Hey, who're you, doll?"

Carol felt herself withdrawing in revulsion. She had to restrain herself from staring.

"You know who I am, doll?" the voice bleated and echoed off the walls, shrill and unnerving. "I'm Mrs. Chico. I'm Mrs. Chico.

I'm Mrs. Chico." The words spun dizzily from her lips, over and over, as though to convince herself.

And then Carol knew. Her glance darted to Jonny.

"Yeah, look at him, doll. He'll tell you who I am. I ain't so nuts, nutsy nuts as all that. Not yet I ain't."

Carol glanced from Jonny back to the poor, raving creature who was his wife. Could this indeed be the woman whose photograph she had seen in the papers with Jonny Chico? The beautiful, blonde daughter of one of New York's most prominent families? It was like Jonny to have married her, to arm himself with a political and social in. She must have provided the respectable front he needed at the start of his double career. And look at her now. Ruined, completely insane. Destroyed, like everything Jonny Chico touched. Maimed for life, like every woman who had loved him.

The room reeked of the heavy cigar pungency.

"A quiet evening at home with Mr. and Mrs.," Jonny said. "I'm entitled to that once in a while, don't you think?"

The cold, hard steel of his words cut through Carol. How could she tell him? How could she apologize?

"I'll go now," Carol mumbled.

"You go nowhere, doll. Not till I give you the word. I got a dead aim with this cigar. One false move from you and bam it goes. You don't tell the coppers nothing, see." She swung a leg over the chair and stood. "Now sit down and behave, dolly doll. I'll call the shots."

Carol knew better than to antagonize her. One false move … If she were so afraid of the police, it must mean that she had, at some time, done something to justify that fear. Something violent. Something that had cost Jonny a lot of sweat to cover up. And if the woman were violent, it must mean that she was normally confined to an institution. One of those fancy places, probably, without walls. Her big shot father would have seen to that. Would probably have seen to it, too, that Jonny never got a chance to forget what he had done to the woman. For if she came here to visit, it was because Jonny needed her to. Because he needed protection. Jonny never did anything for nothing.

No wonder Scrappy had been so overwrought earlier. He must have known...

Slowly, she stepped across to the couch and sat down at the far end, away from Jonny.

Minutes ran by. Scrappy joggled about for a while, then apparently satisfied that all would go smoothly, hopped back into his chair.

"My name's Augusta anyway," the woman muttered into her glass. "Not that you're going to call me anything but Mrs. Chico. He loves me, do y'hear?" she screamed suddenly. "He even sleeps with me sometimes. When the nellie nurse ain't looking. Don't you, hubby? Don't you? Don't you make love with me when the lousy attendant is cruising some sweet little boy?"

Jonny shifted his weight on the cushion. He seemed to Carol limp, drained, as though all the vital machinery inside him had run down. She did not care whether or not what the woman said was true. She cared only that Jonny was fettered to this wreck, for the rest of her life. Whatever his reasons, he would take responsibility for her, would never be able to carve her out of his life—or get the taste of her out of his thoughts.

*And he could never marry me if he wanted to,* she thought. *Even if I got a divorce from George. Life for Jonny and me will always be a matter of back alleys and under the stairs....*

The thought of it made her ill. And yet she couldn't really care. She had come to Jonny, thrown herself at him because she loved him. Because she needed him.

And now, she knew, he needed her. How could it be possible that, of all the women glad to fling themselves at him, die for him, he had wound up with this raving lunatic? He must still need badly the political sanctuary her father could afford him.

Except to save his own neck, Jonny wouldn't go out of his way for anyone.

"Bedtime," Jonny said. "Let Scrappy take you upstairs to bed and I'll be along shortly."

Carol heard the false efficiency in his voice and wondered where he meant to hide the woman. The house had no second floor, she knew. Cautiously, she averted her glance from his face.

"Oh no you don't, cookie. You don't stay here with this doll and send me up there with *him*." Her words leered maliciously. "Either you take me or nobody."

"All right," Jonny said, snapping the words out brittlely. Let's go. And you," he said, turning to Carol, "you are in trouble."

Carl snorted at his back as he disappeared through a doorway with his wife. Little did he know how deeply in trouble she really was.

She sat back then inside the cold misery of her soul, waiting for Jonny to return to her from the upstairs that didn't exist in this house.

# CHAPTER FOURTEEN

"You," she wailed at Scrappy as he sat staring at her glumly. "It's all your fault."

She felt close to tears, closer to a threatening abandon that boded hysteria.

Scrappy shook from side to side, his anger alive and licking through his small body. The dull gleam in his eyes assailed her, tried to ask why she had not done what she was told. His restlessness forced him from the chair. He seemed to be looking for something to break, something to tear or destroy as vent for the pressure of his angry silence.

"You should have told me," Carol rasped. "You could have explained it somehow. Why shouldn't I know about a thing like this when it makes all the difference in the world?"

Scrappy's thick lips twisted. Did it really make a difference? he seemed to ask.

"I don't know ... I don't know ..." Carol spoke more to herself than to Scrappy.

By the time Jonny finally came back into the room, she had subsided into a quiet horror of tomorrow.

"What the hell are you doing here?" Jonny flung at her ferociously.

Carol's shoulders slumped. "If I told you, you'd throw me out," she said.

"I'd throw you out right now if I could," his voice whipped. "But I can't, so you'd better spill it."

"I think I've killed Garril Paterson," Carol said quite simply.

"You what?"

"I hit her over the head with a lamp and drove up here in her car."

"You're dreaming," Jonny said. "Garry doesn't have a car. She can't drive."

Carol stared at him blankly. "Then I've killed her and stolen someone else's car."

Standing just behind Jonny, Scrappy's face contorted with silent laughter.

"Go ahead, both of you," Carol yelled. "Laugh yourselves silly. But it's true. Every word of it." She let her glance fall. "I'm not the crazy one around here, just remember that." Her words were steeped in admonition.

"All right … all *right*," Jonny's voice blanketed hers. "I believe you. Now you'd better start explaining yourself. And fast."

"There's nothing to explain," Carol said quietly. "It's just that I refused to be jailed up. Especially not by you, Jonny Chico. You're the one who's supposed to love me. Then why oh why didn't you trust me enough to tell me about …" she waved one hand helplessly, "… all this."

"That's beside the point," Jonny said. "Now, we've got to get back to town and work out what you said about Garry. First, let's get that car returned. Maybe the owner hasn't missed it yet."

He grabbed Carol's arm and swung her toward the door. "You stay here, Scrap," he said. "We'll be back by morning."

Dragging Carol along, he strode from the house to the car parked in shadows.

"It's Garril's, I swear it," Carol said.

Jonny came to a halt in front of the vehicle. He slid his hands into his pockets and whirled on her. The muscles and bones of his face stood out with jagged strength. "Why, you dumb broad," he laughed harshly. "This is Tom's old Buick. Where in the hell did you get your mitts on it?"

"I tell you, it's Garril's," Carol persisted, knowing she sounded as mad as Jonny's wife. "She drove me home from the bar. We were both a bit polluted and ..."

"Are you sure?"

"Well, how else would I remember it? What would make me suddenly stop on the street and decide that I recognize a car if I never saw it before? Besides, the keys were in the ignition."

"I don't know. I just don't know. But there are a million blue Buicks. Why on earth shouldn't you remember it from somewhere? Maybe some friend of yours had one."

"No, no, no I tell you."

Her conviction barred further question.

"All right," Jonny acquiesced. "Hop in."

"Where are we going?" Carol said, slamming the door.

"To the house, I guess. Where else?"

"Garril's house?"

"Yes."

Carol shuddered. "I can't," she said, rolling up the window. "I couldn't look at it."

Jonny threw the car into gear and shot it out onto the road. "Don't be stupid," he said. "Maybe she isn't dead. What did you do, shoot her?"

"I told you. It was a heavy lamp," Carol said in a low voice.

"Yeah, I know her stuff. But we can't just go on the assumption that you killed somebody unless we know for sure."

"I do know," Carol said. "I feel it in my bones."

Jonny fumbled on the dashboard for the cigarette lighter. "Aw, go on, you don't know anything by now. You're a bundle of nerves. Anyway, even if you did kill the old girl, we've got to return Tom's car. We have to be polite about such things, don't we?"

"Your jokes are in pretty bad taste," Carol said.

"Well, cheer up then so I won't have to kid you along."

"I can't. You make me miserable. I just find it impossible to get it through my head that you intended to keep your wife a secret from me. I'm like a stranger to you. A total stranger."

There was a pause.

"Well, in many ways, dear heart," he said softly, "you are."

"Perhaps you think so for good reason, Jonny. I ran out on you. I didn't write to you while you were in prison. And I married another man. All true. But if you can't put the past aside, what kind of a future can we have?"

"It's not the past that worries me at all," Jonny said. "Nor the future. It's this lousy present. I don't want you to drop your sacred body into hell fires for me, baby. I don't want sacrifices and accusations. There was enough of that from Gussie before she finally cracked her head open. If you can't live happily ever after with me the way I am, my sweet, then let's drop it all right here and now ..." He kept his eyes steadily on the road as he spoke. He might have been mentioning the time of day or the state of the weather. "Right after we see Garry, that is."

Carol felt her toes go numb. Of all the things that she might have expected from him, this sudden cool off was not one of them. Her heart felt as though it were falling through space, dizzily, endlessly downward. The dark wash of shadows on either side of the highway began to take on strange, monstrous shapes. She could say nothing now without sounding like a nag.

"You're looking at it cockeyed, Jonny," was all she could muster. And in a sudden flash of clarity, she could understand why Augusta had gone mad.

She longed for sunlight. But as they hurried through the darkness, Carol wondered if she would get through to see the break of day.

"Whatever you're thinking," Jonny said, "just remember that life is too short for regrets."

"I'm thinking only one thought, Jonny. And that is how I am going to get you to believe that I love you."

Jonny pushed open the vent window and shoved out his cigarette stub. "People don't talk about that kind of thing," he said gruffly. "They demonstrate it."

*Enough,* Carol thought. *Enough punishment for one night.*

She settled into a profound silence that bathed her with warm despair. He would never understand. They weren't speaking the same language any more.

She watched blankly as they approached New York. All capacity to feel seemed crowded into a tiny nugget of loss. Suddenly, she didn't care whether she had killed Garril Paterson or not. A death sentence much more punishing had been laid on her head by Jonny.

"Why don't you just let me out here," Carol said as they paused for a red light on Madison Avenue.

"Why?"

"I'm too tired to go through with this."

"Don't be a fool, girl," Jonny said, catching her by the collar and pulling her back toward him.

Hopefully, she searched his face. "I'd do anything for you, Jonny," she whispered. "Just give me the chance to show it."

"Even murder." He grinned suddenly and the gray stained face took on the young quality she loved.

Slowly, they circled the Paterson house.

"Can't you double park it?" Carol said with a tremor.

"And risk a ticket? Not on your life."

She could not understand his persistent lightheartedness.

"Well, there's no commotion going on," he said, glancing up at the dark windows as they came around for a second time. "Or maybe the cops have come, cleared her away and left without leaving a footprint."

"Jonny."

"Well, what the hell do you expect me to do? The thing that really worries me, I'll tell you, is how you got Tom's car. I mean, he wasn't supposed to be home tonight. In fact, he paid me a great sum in order to keep him happily occupied so he wouldn't have to be home tonight."

Carol felt perversely relieved now that she heard a serious note in Jonny's voice.

"So at least there's something that makes you think," she said with uncontrolled nastiness.

"Few things, but some," he answered, snapping quickly back to his bantering mood.

Finally, they found a shortish space and Jonny angled the car backward. "That'll have to do," he said, coming around to open the door for Carol.

"Out, my little murderer. We've got to return to the scene of the crime."

# CHAPTER FIFTEEN

THE PATERSON house looked too peaceful. Unconsciously, Carol leaned backward as they approached the steps. But Jonny kept her moving forward. He made her look everything straight in the eye, somehow. Even, mysteriously, her own conscience.

"We can't get in," Carol said. "The door's locked from upstairs."

"I see you went through the works," Jonny chuckled and pressed the door bell.

An eternity passed as they waited. Then the knob turned. The door opened.

"I don't care if I never see you two again as long as I live," Garril said from underneath an enormous ice bag. She turned abruptly and started back into the hallway. Her woolen bathrobe swung with energy.

A dam inside Carol burst. She felt the rise of hot tears moving up rapidly. Her body limp, she let her head fall against Jonny's sleeve. She clung to his arm and hung on while the hot sobs twisted out of her.

"And where, for heaven's sake, is Tom?" Garril's voice leaped at them from the adjoining living room.

Jonny pushed Carol inside. "That's what I came to ask you," he called back to the voice.

"All this fun and games is lousing him up, Jonny Chico."

"He's a big boy, Garry. Let him call his own shots, will you?" Chico said.

Carol tried to stop her ears against the yelling going back and forth around her head. They seemed insane, all of them. Bouncing around like happy rubber toys. Nothing seemed to stop them. Nothing made them pause to think. She took the handkerchief that Jonny thrust at her while he shouted at Garril. She pressed the linen to her eyelids and forced the tears back to where they belonged, hidden.

"Oh, shut your fool face and come have a drink," Garril said at last. "And bring your little tiger with you."

"I can't face her," Carol whispered to Jonny.

"Nonsense." He shoved her ahead of him into the room.

The cigarette butts, emptied bottles and general party debris were still strewn about as Carol remembered from the night George had brought her here.

"Ginger ale, beer or milk? Somebody's getting neglectful about the refreshments around here," Garril said apologetically.

"No one gives a damn about your housekeeping." Jonny said.

"Or my son," Garril said, pulling the robe tighter. "Or me," she concluded, giving a mock glare at Carol. But I'll tell you it was worth it," she grinned at Jonny. "Almost."

Carol felt her face go purple.

Garril let herself flop to soft cushions. She sighed with a faint tone and readjusted the pack on her head. "The drinks are in the small fridge," she said, pointing across the room while she shut her eyes.

"We're not here for fun, Garry," Jonny's voice was clipped. "I want to know how my friend here got Tom's car."

"So do I," Garril said. "But not while my heart aches like this."

"I'm sorry," Carol murmured.

They were ignoring her but she had to get a word in. It irritated her, somehow, that they seemed to know each other so well. It had nothing to do with her, had happened while Chico was out of her life. Yet the intimacy between them sent prickles of jealousy chasing down her spine. And she understood how Tom must have felt, being so close and always an outsider. He must hate Chico. He must hate her, for loving Chico. He must be nearly mad with his hate.

"Let me use your phone," Jonny said. "I'll see if I can track him down through the girls."

He raked through a pile of crumpled napkins to a telephone on a small walnut table. The women remained silent while he dialed half a dozen numbers and hung up from each abruptly. Carol could see that he ran his organization with the efficiency of a man in politics. Despite herself, it sent a chill of disgust through her. Now, razor-sharp, energetic and curt, he reminded her of the big-time mobster type that she had seen in second-rate films. A curtain seemed to lift from over her eyes. She saw Jonny for the first time as a user of human flesh. An elaborate parasite.

Forcibly, she pushed the image from her thoughts.

"And what if he doesn't find Tom?" Carol said to Garril. "Is it necessarily any of his business?"

Garril smiled to herself. She didn't bother to open her eyes. "There's a lot here that doesn't meet the eye, my child. But give yourself time. You'll get the hang of it."

Carol pondered Garril's words, wondering if she really were so eager to get the hang of it. She considered the vast number of surprises still in store for her and tried to believe that some of them might be pleasant.

Jonny finally dropped the receiver into its cradle with a definitive plop.

"Forget it," he said to no one in particular. He went to stand at the window, legs spread, hands deep in pockets, neck taut as he stared between the heavy curtains at what Carol thought must be a lightening sky.

Garril said, "I think the Paterson family is due for a refund this year."

"Very funny," Jonny said without turning around.

Garril shrugged.

Then an exclamation came from Jonny's lips. The exact words were muffled within the fever of his momentary surprise. He turned from the curtains but stood there quite still. His angry features began to recompose, filing into a soldierly order of alert serenity. The transformation shook Carol. She stared at him, hoping for some hint.

"Prepare yourself, sweetie," he said to her, "for old home week."

Before Carol could voice a question, the front door opened.

"Anybody up?" Paterson's voice searched. "We've got company for breakfast."

Paterson marched into the room, his well-kept body erect but his walk stiff with exhaustion. The masses of white hair fell disheveled over his forehead and the tie knot hung slightly loosened from his collar.

"Well, well," Paterson said, "a good night was had by all, I see." Smiling with subtle triumph, he brought George Trace around into the room beside him.

"Carol."

Her name sounded dead on his lips. His thin physique, once so supple, so elastic, seemed brittle now. As though his bones had dried out inside his skin and would blow away. His face had grown somehow longer and his glasses were two squares of vapor that he lifted off, revealing puffy, irritated eyes.

"You look great," Garril said, "both of you."

Carol wished she were dead. She didn't want to look at George, didn't want to see him like this. Her picture of him without her had seemed so pleasant before. She had left him free to devote himself to science. He should look grateful, alive, expansive as he had been that night in the cab. But he looked as dead as she wished she was.

"Well, Tom," Jonny said. "Garry's been telling me I owe you both a refund."

"Oh?" Paterson said, opening the refrigerator and taking out the bottles of milk.

"For services not rendered," Carol intruded. She needed to see if she could still speak. Or if she had really fallen into the pit of her own stomach.

"Is that so?" Paterson said inquiringly to Garril.

Carol saw how they were all ignoring George. He had been the belle of the ball that one night and how the star had faded—no longer a novelty for the thrill seekers, she supposed. He had amused them for a few hours and now he was finished. She wondered if Garril had been cruel enough to change her mind about the grant.

And Paterson. Why had he brought George here?

Suddenly, Carol began to see Tom Paterson in a different light. Petty blackmail, Garril had said. Sadism would have been more like it. Obviously, he had brought George here to show him what his wife was really like. Not bad enough that George should know she had run off with Jonny Chico—to really smear his face in the mud ... show him his wife in bed with another woman. He could crush George that way. Could destroy anyone but Jonny Chico, the man he hated. Jonny would laugh in his face.

But some day Tom would even the score with Chico. Some day ...

Jonny leaned slightly back against the curtains. "Tom, I set up an appointment for you last night. What happened?"

"Nothing," Tom said easily. "I kept it, of course. What do you want, bugles?"

"You kept it," Jonny repeated.

"Yes, that's what I said."

"Well, it so happens," Jonny paused to take the glass of milk Tom put into his hand, "that I was phoning around town looking for you. I didn't get the idea that you were where I thought you would be."

Tom waited. He seemed to be surveying the level manner, the mild, yet pointed inquiry. "That's my privilege," he said just as quietly.

"Of course," Jonny conceded.

"But I didn't intend to scratch it off the bill," Tom said with a new-found geniality. "You supplied the more than adequate services," he continued pleasantly. "And I chose to dispense with them as I saw fit. Okay? Everyone satisfied?"

Carol, watching the performance, felt instant revulsion for the grin that seemed to be taking in the whole room.

"George and I," Tom continued, "were talking business of ... another nature."

Carol looked to George's face for corroboration.

*Lies,* Carol thought. *The room is full of lies.*

"Can we go now, Jonny?" she said meekly.

In three steps, George was beside her. "You'd better get hold of yourself," he grabbed her jacket sleeve. "You'd better think about it and make up your mind that what you're doing is crazy." His lips were pale and cracked.

"Let go of her," Jonny said with a drawling casualness.

"Think about it," George rasped. His eyeballs jutted close to Carol's face. "Just think about it."

"I said, let go." With a lightning motion, Jonny spun him away.

Physically, George was no match for him, Carol knew. Years of bending over microscopes and working with laboratory equipment had scaled him down to finer muscular adjustments. And obviously, he had been up all night with Tom.

"She's still my wife," George said, lunging desperately at Jonny.

Jonny held him off with one hand. "Take it easy," he said.

"You bastard. You son of a bitch coward," George screamed. He swung a fist that connected with Jonny's shoulder. The blow moved Jonny a little.

"Hey," Tom called gleefully. "None of that. No jealous cock fights in this house."

But to Carol, Tom seemed relieved that the focus of attention had shifted away from himself. Relieved … and what else? What was it she sensed about him? A hatred, an anger, directed at both the struggling men. It made no sense to her.

"Jonny, please," Carol added, afraid that George would wind up smashed into a corner. "I want to go home." Purposely, intuitively, she ignored George, knowing that any encouragement from her would only rouse him further.

She ran forward and grabbed Chico's arm.

Fighting desperately, she managed to drag him toward the door and push him out onto the street.

The cold morning air hit them both. Wet, nasty and gray, it drowned out Carol's moment of spirit. She stood trembling now as the chill reached through her.

"I hope you're satisfied," she said woodenly. "Everybody's humiliated now because of you. Did you expect George to act any differently, seeing me again? And Tom, did you have to open him up in front of the whole world and show what a useless pile of dollars he is? Jonny, Jonny, you're like a rotten fish that makes everything it touches stink to high heaven. Can't you even see that poor Garril loves you, too? Can't you see that she takes women from you just to be near you without hurting her pride too much? She doesn't need to pay for it, Jonny. What is it with you? Why does everybody get suddenly so unlucky near you while you ride high above the mess? Why, Jonny? …"

Carol heard herself raving but she felt powerless to stop. The pressure of her thoughts had pushed the top of her head off, it seemed. And as she sank herself into the rapidly spilling words, a perverse ointment of pleasure began to smooth over the torn and open hurts that raked at her heart.

"That's quite an opinion you have," Jonny said evenly. He turned up his jacket collar against the dawn. "I guess I've put you through too much, these past couple of days. Come on, I'll take you back and you can take plenty of time pulling yourself together."

Carol leaned rigidly backward. "I don't want you to take me to that horrid little room. I don't want you to drop me off like a bag of beans and leave me there. I need to be with you, Jonny. If I wanted to be alone, I could have stayed with George."

The words had slipped out of her, but now that they were said, she felt glad.

"All right," Jonny conceded. He seemed suddenly tired. "I'll stay with you."

What did she really want? Carol asked herself riding back with him in the cab in silence. She felt all wrong, forcing Jonny to stay with her. She didn't want to have to plead with him.

Upstairs in the small room again, she sat him down on the bed and put herself close beside him. Morning hovered above them, filtering through the skylight softly. Jonny lay back on the pillow and clasped his hands behind his neck. She watched him gazing at the shafts of light. The shine seemed slightly duller in his eyes now, the tension that made of his face a vital force had ebbed perceptibly

*I'm boring him,* she thought wildly. And all the questions, all the demands about the blood stains in the closet, about his wife, about the person who could be following him, fled.

She knew only that she must capture him again. Must enchant him, bring forth the fire in him without which she felt she could not live.

She lifted his legs onto the bed and began untying his shoe laces. "Let's forget everything," she said softly, "and just be us. Together."

Her fingers were cold and stiff from the night, from her reactions, but she started to massage his feet, moving slowly down the sole to the arch. One thing in her favor, she realized—she remembered his idiosyncracies. Yes, she knew what he liked.

How he loved being touched and kneaded, his sensuous cravings brought alive by moving, rhythmic contact.

Carol took off her skirt quickly, giving her legs room to straddle him at the slim width of his hips. She pulled his shirt out and moved her hands up along his skin.

"Your fingers are cold," he said.

She heard the growing pleasure in his voice and felt encouraged.

Leaning forward, she breathed warmth on his neck and put the weight of her body on her hands, warming them with her own heat. She moved her knees down along his thighs and pressed them in, working her whole body on him.

"I'll warm you up," she whispered, closing her eyes for one delicious second to envision the process of their love-making.

Carol stretched herself out on top of him now and rubbed her belly along his back. She reached under herself and grabbed the hard flanks of him, massaging upward into the small of his spine. She heard him groan into the pillow and smiled a little, knowing that he could be hers if she would only work hard enough at keeping him. Gradually, she lowered her mouth to the bristles of hair at his neck and ran the tip of her tongue across from one ear to the other, inhaling the odor of him that brought her awake, tightened her senses, made her thankful again to be alive and aware of her own voluptuous body.

She felt her breasts leaping like spring buds inside her brassière as she clung to him and pressed herself harder to his body. Reaching along the buttons of his shirt, she got it off him and laid her cheek against the pattern of muscles on his back.

"Come here," he said roughly and turning over, slid her to the mattress.

Carol helped him get her clothes off. She heard her slip tearing as he pulled it and she clawed to tear it further still, hardly able to wait for the skin-real contact of their bodies.

"I need you," she whispered. "Make me feel you ... all of you."

And she slithered her hips upward, searching for him.

"You always rush things," he said, pulling away.

"Don't make me suffer, Jonny, please..." Her hands groped to him, to hold his largeness, the virile reality that gave her strength, that made her dig deeply for hope in the wreckage of her life.

Carol felt his body give in to her desire. She felt the contractions in his legs convulsing upward, sending waves of motion to her, throbbing and caressing her body. She grasped him to her with her limbs, to make him one with her, contacting always their point of mutual ecstasy.

The room around her began to rock. Her lips burned with drying perspiration that came and went. She soaked her nostrils in the closeness of him, tasted the beginning roughness of his chin, rubbed herself up and down the smooth hardness pressing to her.

*Love me forever,* she said to him silently. *Keep me... use me.*

Her nails dug into his shoulders and slid down along his back. She was drawing blood, she knew, yet she could not stop herself. A molten need to blend herself into him sent liquid flames of desire to the very ends of her being.

*Why can't you always be good like this... good to me... good...*

"Oh, so good," she moaned aloud, her thoughts and words blending now unconsciously.

And she held him tight, swaying with him and slapping the great crests of her desire into peaks of burning foam.

"Say it," she cooed, "say it."

Jonny spat the single word into her ear, then repeated it softly, lengthily, creating for her the image of what they were doing. It was as though she could catch their act from all sides, a spectator at her own desire, as many mirrors reflect a single image.

The pains of the past liquified and drained away.

Like a goddess she strode in giant steps across the heights of fabulous mountains.

Then dizzily, she plummeted, falling rapidly down a cylinder of darkness. Her voice gasped on an intake of breath. Her skin seemed to burst into flame.

Her body became a single, quickening pulse beating around and inside her. Overwhelming her, then slowing, slowing as she drifted gently, featherlike, swinging gradually back to earth.

She felt the pillow crushed between her shoulder-blades. The shaft of daylight lay on their nakedness.

"Jonny," she whispered, "why can't it always be like this?"

She watched him smile a tiny twist of salty amusement. "Because, my little Bittersweet," he said, "we weren't born yesterday."

# CHAPTER SIXTEEN

S HE LAY on the bed, expansive and liquid-feeling in her pleasure. The smoke from her cigarette shivered upward, design-
ing puffs and swirls in the lightly moving air. Her brain felt like a
sponge filled to capacity. She could not think, but only feel the tip
sensations of her nerves as though snapped back through millions of years to mute animal awareness.

She felt Jonny moving and without looking at him, knew that
he sat up.

He padded about the room, picking up pieces of his clothing.
His familiar motions of getting dressed happened in silence.

Minutes later she heard from behind her the faucets turned
on and then off again.

When he returned to the room, he stood before her neat and
fully dressed.

He stood at the foot of the bed, his face calmed. "I've got to
go now," he said.

"No," she said simply.

"I'm sorry, Carol, but I've got to."

"No, Jonny," she repeated. Her voice rose high. "I don't want
you to leave me again."

"Don't be silly, honey."

"Jonny, please."

She saw his lips tighten with impatience. But he couldn't run
off again. She couldn't stand all the senseless, violent things that
happened when he left her. Together, they found peace. Beauty,

even. But apart, the world seemed to go mad—shattering itself into jagged pieces that cut her.

"Then take me with you."

He shook his head. "Try to understand," he said.

"I won't understand." She felt a rising desperation. "I can't." She catapulted up from the bed and reached to grab him.

Jonny stepped back out of her grasp.

"Look," he said, "I've got to get back to the house. It may be hard for you to realize it, but I left an irresponsible woman out there to come with you."

"Scrappy can take care of her."

Jonny paused. His eyelids lowered, closing him away from her. "She's my responsibility," he said. "I've got to answer to her old man for what happens to her. And he knows when she comes home to visit. Why do you suppose—"

"Why can't I come then?" she interrupted. "She won't see me. I'll stay in the kitchen or under the couch until you get rid of her." She paused at the sound of her own words. "You *are* going to *send* her back, aren't you?"

She watched him start to say something. But then, apparently changing his mind, he turned and strode from the room, leaving her to dangle on the breaking limb of her desperate helplessness.

For a while she lay quite still, feeling a bitter taste rise burning in her throat. The walls around her seemed to be expanding as though she lay in the airless center of an opaque balloon floating her away, far away toward destruction.

She dashed from the bed and ran naked to the door.

"Jonny," she called up the stairs. "Jonny." Her voice went raw on the name. She heard the two syllables split and break away, resounding between her ears.

Her knees began to quiver. The waves of weakness ran up through her thighs. She felt herself slipping, slipping till she lay on the floor.

And sobbing there in the doorway, knowledge burst on her. She understood what the blood in the closet meant. How easy for a woman to try to kill herself, rather than go through the pain of loving him. Of loving him, but never quite reaching him, feeling him slipping away on the silken route of his nonchalance. And she realized that it must have been Augusta, his wife, the one woman who had probably suffered the most. Augusta, who had loved him once … who loved him still.

She pressed her face against the wooden doorframe and slowly began hitting her forehead against it. No use … no use … no use ….

But then a cold shaft of light pierced her hot despair. She wasn't Augusta. She was stronger than Augusta. She would not let Jonny Chico drive her mad, push her to the point of violence.

The sobs turned dry and she pulled herself back to her feet.

She dressed slowly and with care.

The meticulous matron in control. With all her strength, Carol reached for the mask that had steadied her through seven years. She felt it begin to lower, mercifully, over her feelings.

When she had combed her hair and put on makeup, she looked in the mirror and saw a strong, self-possessed woman, a regal face to which nothing but pleasantries had happened since the day of her birth.

Minutes later she was out on the street and looking for a telephone booth.

She looked for and found the Paterson number, then dialed it with steady, iced fingers.

"Tom? … Yes, Carol Trace …. Tom, I want you to do something for me." She spoke with command, with conviction, as though a piece of displaced memory had clicked into place. "I want you to drive me up to Jonny's house. Will you do that?"

Yes, of course, He'd be delighted.

"In five minutes? I'll be at the corner of Madison and Fifty-seventh."

When she hung up, Carol bought a package of peppermint Life Savers and put one on her tongue. But she didn't taste the flavor.

A struggling sun hung behind stretches of cloud. Wind played at her skirt and slid under her collar. People walked around her. A man jostled her as he hastened to cross against a light. She hardly felt him and barely heard his apology as she stared at the cars coming around the block.

She saw Paterson's leather brown face above the steering wheel and she waved.

He pulled up to the curb and she hopped in before he had stopped completely.

"Aren't we in a hurry?" he said, peering in the rearview mirror to make a U-turn.

She didn't answer him. The force behind her convictions did not need words for expression. This once she felt sure of herself. Rock certain. *This is how Johnny feels,* she thought, *when he meets a woman.*

"A woman scorned," Tom rattled on, "is a python, a tempest, a scourge of nature. Beware the woman scorned."

"Will you hurry?" she said, her voice low.

"For you, my dear? Wife of the eminent chemist, pretender to the Nobel throne by proxy, lover of Prince Valiant himself. Yes, for you I will not only hurry, but I will step on it."

He wasn't drunk, she knew, but he was high on something. Maybe lack of sleep. Maybe the dregs of his own uselessness.

"I will step on it and you will provide me with a show worth watching from an orchestra seat, won't you, my dear? You will display for me the extremes of human capacity seldom witnessed in civilization. You will show me all this and I am therefore your humble servant. Some collect the varicolored butterfly, but I? I collect the varicolored human specimen..."

Carol didn't try to stop his rattling. His words were but a faint buzz on the outskirts of her own thought.

And the car sped arrowlike to the bull's-eye of her target.

# CHAPTER SEVENTEEN

S HE HAD never seen the house without shadow. In the pale daylight, it seemed somehow small, somehow lower as though hugging onto the earth for fear of slipping off.

Or was it her own projection, Carol wondered. Was she afraid now of slipping off the spinning whirlagig that had held out a promise to her? Was she afraid that it must all come to a halt and send her home again, like a child leaving the large wonders of a circus to return once more to cereal where there had been cotton candy?

But she must not think of this. She must do what she had to do. And whatever the consequences, she would face them, admit them, welcome them as part of the pattern of her destiny.

"And so, Mrs. Trace," Tom beamed in on her thoughts, "we are here. What now?"

What, indeed.

"We're going inside, of course," she said flatly and swung out of the car.

"And what will you find inside to please you?" he persisted, standing beside her now, his wrinkled face all smiles as though over afternoon tea. "A madwoman, a twisted little misfortune of nature and the black Mephistopheles. A wicked broth."

Carol's shoes sank into the graveled path. How did Tom Paterson know they would find Augusta there? Surely Jonny wouldn't have told him. "How much you know," she said with a flick of curiosity, "about Jonny's private affairs."

"He interests me."

"Yes," Carol said, her voice intense with sudden meaning, "I know."

She watched for Paterson's reaction and felt satisfied to see one thick eyebrow twitch in unexpected consternation. "And you interest me," she said.

Then she spun away from him and proceeded toward the house that looked so harmless and peaceful with glimmerings of sunlight beginning to play on the blue slate shingles.

Carol knew what she had to do. Really, she had known it all along but not until now could she face the truth. She must walk into that house, filled with madness and secrets, and demand that Jonny give her a permanent place in his life. She must demand, and with straightforwardness, that he acknowledge her in front of everyone. For she could not live like the other women who had flitted through his life.

Without Jonny and his love, she was nothing. Less than a shadow. A cursed thing waiting for dispensation of his favor.

And as such, she could not survive.

"You know what you're doing," Paterson's voice blew toward her from behind. "You know the bite of the snakes in that pit."

Carol's shoulders felt stiff as they pulled her along, leading her to Jonny ... and the choice that Jonny would make.

She paused for a moment on the threshold. Her nostrils widened and she drew in a short breath of air. It tasted fresh with a brown, earth odor. Carol knew that she would always remember this odor, this touch of fertility and goodness even here, even in this place.

There were no doorbells on Jonny's house. The door would either open to her touch or she would force her way in. Perhaps break a window.

She turned the knob.

And the door yielded before her.

A radio blasted a deep, breathy voice, a news commentator. She almost smiled, jolted by the awareness that other things were going on besides her own fate.

The loud voice covered her footsteps.

She appeared at the doorway of the living room. And for an instant she stood there, surveying the three people who did not yet know she watched them.

There were tears running down Gussie's flaccid cheeks. "I can't go back," she was saying. "Not in the middle of the week." Her voice screeched hen-like, shrill and clear above the radio. "Jonny, sweetsie doll, you promised me I could come home some day. You said it. Yes you did. You did. You did."

Jonny stood beside the radio. For once his calm face held a touch of color.

And Scrappy hovered beside the woman, his eyes jolting almost out of their sockets watching her.

"Good-day to all," Paterson said.

The three heads swiveled to Paterson and Carol in the archway. Jonny snapped off the radio.

"Jesussake," he said.

"Now, be nice," Paterson's voice became oiled. "Be a gentleman and welcome your guests with politeness, my friend."

Gussie grabbed the sides of her chair. Her pointed nails went into them and pulled deep tears in the material.

"Traitor. Lousy traitor," she screamed at Jonny.

"Mrs. Chico, how do you do," Tom continued, ignoring her remark. "Do you think I'm a policeman? That I've come to get you? Do you think your husband fooled you?"

Scrappy hopped closer to the woman. Her hair swung forward into her face. She spat past Scrappy's shoulder. "To hell with you all," she squawked. "I can take care of myself. Whore. Tramp. Sonofa sonofa..." Her voice spluttered away.

"I'm sorry, Jonny," Carol said. "But we've got to have a little truth around here."

"What kind of truth do you want?" he yelled. "What kind of havoc, you stupidassed female? Can't you see what I've got here?"

His thrust barely touched Carol's wounds. She felt a mild sensation of surprise at the numbness surrounding her. "Yes, I can see," she said, her voice barely audible. "But you never wanted to help me to see, did you?"

"We are policemen in a way, aren't we?" Paterson said, eyeing Gussie furtively.

"In a way," Carol said. "I've come, you might say, Jonny, for your statement."

"Oh, for chrissakes get the hell out of here till later." He knocked one fist backward against the wall.

"I'm tired of later," Carol said.

"Cops? Jonny called the cops? On me? His wife? His very own wife?"

Gussie started up from the chair, lunging forward.

Instantly, Scrappy jumped in front of her. He grabbed her wrists. The strength of him flung her back, bounced her into the chair. Her head hit the soft cushioned back. "Lousy, lousy traitor," her voice cracked.

"That seems to be the opinion of many in this room," Paterson said mildly. "Yes, the opinion of many."

"All right, Scrappy, take it easy," Jonny said, his voice trembling to stay under control. "I'll call the hospital."

"Hospital? You sonofabitch. Don't want no ..." Kicking her sneakered feet, Gussie struggled up, forcing Scrappy backward with the giant-like strength derived from her terror. Her widened eyes were shot through with red. Her lids fluttered like a dying bird.

"I'll help you, Scrappy, old man," Paterson said, striding forward.

Carol saw Paterson press himself against the woman. She saw him deliberately push her hand into the pocket of his jacket.

Gussie's hand emerged with a gun gripped in the claws of its tightening grasp.

Scrappy flung himself against her as the first shot exploded through the house. A second and a third pumped into him, jerking his small frame like a puppet string, pulling him up as he sank, then letting him fall again.

He slipped away to the floor, dragging a path of blood along the glistening lamé skirt.

"One down," Gussie screamed. "One stinking traitor down."

Patterson slipped behind her and behind the chair.

Carol didn't move. She could only look at Jonny and remember how nice it had been once, how cool and how warm under the heavy spring foliage with him.

"Next pigeon," Gussie rasped. "Next traitor down to hell."

Jonny was coming at her fast and the bullet caught him in the center of a stride. He stood in mid-air for an instant as though the subject of an action photograph. Then the run slowed to a walk. He took a step and another faltering step. Then he stood still. A grin appeared on his lips. As they tilted upward, so debonair, blood spilled over and slid down his chin.

Then he began sitting down. Very slowly. Almost as though he were moving toward a chair.

He hit the floor abruptly hard.

"And last of all, the number one jerk."

The sound of Gussie's raving was cut off in the blast of the final shot.

Carol heard it but didn't even look to see.

Her gaze remained riveted on Jonny, who was looking up at her, refusing even now to let the smile fade.

"You look so damned ..." he struggled for a breath, "... sexy up there."

And the grin stayed with Jonny Chico as he toppled sideways to the carpet.

# CHAPTER EIGHTEEN

Through the sudden stillness, she heard the telephone clicking.

"Operator, the police, please." Patterson's voice resounded with a deep gravity.

Carol sat down on the couch. She waited till he had replaced the receiver.

"Strange, the ways of love," he said mildly, drawing a cigarette case from inside his jacket. "This has been a very instructive day for me."

Carol knew that she could not close her eyes and force him to dissolve just because she willed it. "I need some air," she said. Her knees felt hot and cold, yet the rest of her felt nothing. Her eyes seemed to be in a temporary state of blindness like one who comes into a glaring light from utter dark.

"By all means," Patterson said. "But don't roam too far. The police will be needing us both for questions."

Carol didn't bother to answer him. She stumbled toward the door and pushed her way outside.

Of them all, she felt most sorry about Scrappy. The little man, in his blind devotion to Jonny Chico, had paid with his life. And yet it was inevitable she supposed. Jonny had always had the taint of death and destruction and decay about him. Everything he had ever touched had turned to dust. Except herself. In a way, she had been lucky.

She began suddenly to shiver and her teeth chattered loudly inside her head. Crossing her arms, she held herself close and squinted out across the wide expanse of flat gilded clouds absorbing a strengthening sun. Fragments of scattered blue were becoming defiantly visible. A sparrow twittered somewhere in the woods far behind the pool. A great wave of fatigue rolled through her.

She strolled over to the old Buick and thoughtfully drew a finger along the adhesive patch across one headlight.

Then, from the hills she heard a siren slice through the silence. It reached her ears, yet strangely she felt certain that it could not reach deep enough to penetrate her own vast calm.

A thickly built man in plain clothes escorted her back to the house. He brought her around to the kitchen and sat her down on a red wooden chair.

Without asking her a question, he found a bottle and poured some of the contents into a glass. He steadied her hands around the glass and helped her bring it to her lips.

And then it began. The routine.

Questions.

Voices resounding through the tin hall of her brain.

Answers.

"No, I didn't see. No, I didn't see. No, I didn't ..."

*I was looking at Jonny all the time. I didn't care who she killed. I just was looking at Jonny to see what he looked like when he didn't love me any more.*

"Never saw her ... didn't know her ... hadn't seen him since after high school ..."

*He had to die. I knew he had to die. He couldn't go on doing what he did to us and not die someday.*

"I had no idea she was violent. No, I don't know what hospital ..."

*Scrappy knew about Tom all along. Of course he did. He couldn't tell me because Jonny wouldn't have wanted me to do something silly. What could be sillier than ... all this?*

"Thank you, Mrs. Trace. The officer will drive you home."

With the sirens screaming and bursting through her spongy skull, they reached Park Avenue.

Did she have a key? The doorman would let her in.

Silently polite, the officer rode up with her in the elevator.

He opened the door for her. "You ought to have somebody with you," he said. "Want me to call your husband?"

Carol shook her head. "I can take care of that, thank you."

Wordlessly he pulled the door shut between them.

And now she was alone in the apartment, Mrs. George Trace.

*I ought to want to open a window and throw myself out.*

She went to the window in the kitchen—the window with the view of New York splintering along the sky. She opened the window. A gust of smoky air blew in, prickling her nostrils with its pungency. The smell of automobiles fighting through traffic. The smell of factories she couldn't see. The smell of people sweating to live. Poor, wizened people with nothing to look forward to except tomorrow.

Nothing but tomorrow.

Carol sat down on the window sill and brought her gaze back from the expanse of city and into the kitchen.

Pots and dishes and a yellow stain around the sink.

She had left it like this. When? An eternity ago. A few days. Always. She had always left the kitchen dirty. The back room that nobody saw but she and George. And George had never said anything to her about it.

George must be at the lab.

He would always go to the lab and find his friends at the far end of a microscope. Perhaps he slept there now. She envied anybody who could sleep.

Mechanically, she went to the phone on the wall.

"Garril? ... Garry, you've got to know something about Tom. I've got a long story to tell you and I've got to tell you the whole thing till it's ended the right way."

All right. Garril would catch a cab as soon as she got dressed.

Carol let the receiver dangle and wandered through the empty rooms. Circling slowly, she moved inch by inch toward George's bedroom.

She stepped over the threshold and blinked down at the rumpled bed. At the squashed pillows that had held Jonny's weight, the twisted sheets that had responded to her passion.

A jolt of energy blazed through her and she ripped off the sheet, pulled free the pillowcases, ran with them to the hall incinerator.

Pacified, she put on a fresh set of linen. George's bed looked so pristine now. Almost virginal. He had been a virgin when they married and she remembered how she had laughed at him silently in the night and called him fool.

She laughed now and the laughter turned into a choking sob.

Carol flung her body onto the bed and clutched one pillow close, twisting it in her anguish beneath the welling of her tears.

And her tears rode smooth as a Christmas sled into dreamless sleep.

Sleep.

Somewhere very far away, Carol felt the touch of a hand on her shoulder. It did not try to shake her awake. It simply lay there for some moments, making contact, transfusing life back into her. She remained very still, trying to reach out toward that hand with her mind. She felt suspended in feathery darkness, drugged and unable to move from the center of her deep abyss.

Then the hand lifted.

Carol struggled with the weights on her eyelids, struggled to lift them off. She heard a sigh, her own sigh escaping from dry lips too brittle to form words.

"You aren't sleeping any more," a voice said. "Try to open your eyes, Carol. Try."

The voice reached toward her with the same friendliness as the hand that lingered on her shoulder.

*Try.*

"You can't go on sleeping," the voice persisted. "You must wake up and face whatever it is that's troubling you."

The voice itself did not sound troubled.

*Am I troubled? ... I'm sleepy ... Can't wake up ...*

"Try."

The presence of this person in the room with her was becoming sharper. She heard footsteps across the rug. She heard the trickle of something being poured into a glass. She heard a chair being moved to the side of the bed.

Drops of cool water touched her cheeks. Then her forehead.

Carol tried to turn her head away.

"You're not asleep," the voice persisted. "So open your eyes and look at me."

A long sigh shivered from her.

"That's right. Talk. Talk to me."

*I can talk if I don't have to open my eyes. I know I can talk. But I don't want to see. I don't want to look at the daylight. Or the nighttime.*

"You phoned to tell me something. Now I want to hear it, Carol."

With effort, Carol opened her eyes.

"Garry?"

The name was hardly more than a mumble.

"Yes, I'm right here, darling. Waiting."

"I'm ... sorry I ... hit ..."

"That's done with, Carol. I've forgotten it already. You only did what you had to do."

A light breath of relief blew through Carol as she heard the forgiveness.

"Now, tell me all about it. You've been sleeping for almost two days and you've got to wake up."

"I want to tell you," Carol said, the words coming more easily now. "Will you believe me?"

"Of course."

Carol bit her lip. "Jonny is ..."

"Yes, I know," Garril said.

A damp cloth came to lie on Carol's forehead. Its coolness seemed to draw out some of the pain.

"It was Tom's fault ... do you know ... Tom brought ..."

"Yes, somehow she got his gun. I know it all, Carol. That's not what you wanted to tell me, is it?"

Carol shook her head. "He did it purposely," she said.

"Now what does that mean?" Garril said gently.

"Tom killed ..."

Carol paused. She sensed a nervousness, felt it vibrating from a far corner of the room.

"Go on," Garril urged. The calm, encouraging tone had fallen away. It was only a thin veil now, covering an exploded inner tension.

Still with her eyes closed, Carol listened. Then she heard it, a faint shuffling away at a distance.

Suddenly, she knew that Garril was not the only one in the room with her.

Her eyelids opened, moving with reflex action.

"Yes, Carol, go on," Tom said from where he leaned on the window sill. "Tell Mother all your nightmares and get rid of them." His voice was superficially paternal, but the wrinkles in his face had frozen deep as though etched with acid.

"It's true," Carol yelled at him, "and you know it."

"Of course, dear," he said. Then to Garril, "She may be having a nervous breakdown. Maybe we'd better call a doctor."

Carol's glance flicked from Tom to Garril. She searched Garril's face and found in it confusion.

"You don't believe me?" Carol said weakly. "You think I'm having hallucinations."

"I don't know," Garril said. "How should I know which of you to believe?"

Carol sat up from the pillows. She needed to run away. Get out of this room, away from these people to where she could think. Maybe it was true. Maybe she had made it up in the depths of her dream.

But no. She could see it still. Over and over with the vividness of life, she could see the whole horrible moment again.

She flung the blanket away and bounded out of the bed. George's pajamas fluttered loosely. The long pants tripped her as she tried to walk.

"Just get back into bed," Tom said.

He grabbed her wrist and pulled her back.

"If you weren't guilty," Carol said, "you wouldn't be so damned scared of me."

The truth of it resounded through the room. She watched Tom's cheeks go pale beneath the tan.

"You'd be scared, too," Tom answered, "if someone were trying to accuse you falsely. With circumstantial evidence."

Carol didn't try to answer. How could she match Tom's ability at evasion? How could she match the money he had for spending on legal advice.

Besides, it was perfectly true. All the evidence she had was purely circumstantial.

"No one could possibly believe you," Tom said. "You'd better give it up and try to forget the whole horrible mess."

Carol took one final look at Garril.

"He's right," Garril said gently. "And most sensible."

Carol fell back against the pillows and closed her eyes, needing to block out the sight of the two impersonal faces, so strange, so far away from her.

*Jonny… Jonny, there's no way I can help you… No way I can free myself from the burden of your murder.*

# CHAPTER NINETEEN

S HE WOULD go away.

No clothing, no money, no destination.

Just walk out of the house and into oblivion to live out her years as best she could far from the events, if not from the memory of them.

Maybe even change her name.

Now that they had left her, she could get out of bed and dress. The sleeve of George's pajama top dangled crazily over her fingers.

Carol stood up and pulled at the pants cord. She watched them drop around her ankles. A faint heat of embarrassment rose as she tried to remember who had changed her. Was it Garril?

Her shoulders ached. Stiffness rose along one side of her neck. The fog of confusion had lifted from her brain, leaving her physically depleted.

She needed to soak it all out of her. A good hot bath, a cup or two of black coffee would bring her around sufficiently to get moving.

Carol went into the bathroom and turned on the faucets, listening to the comfortable gurgling as the water swirled and welled over the closed drain. It was a big tub—old-fashioned— built for reclining. She reached over to the soap dish and dropped the heavy oval cake into the water.

While the tub filled, she could put up a kettle for the coffee.

It seemed like a long trip through the many rooms to the kitchen. Odd pieces of furniture she had never noticed before called her attention now. She saw the faded back rest of George's chair, the dust on two porcelain statues they'd brought home one summer from Italy.

So many yesterdays.

Carol pushed open the door of the kitchen and stepped in.

"Hello."

George didn't try to smile. Scruffles of beard made his face heavier around the chin. Older.

"You?"

"Why not?" he said simply and rubbed a cigarette butt into the pile heaped and spilling from a saucer. "I live here too, you know."

She didn't have the strength to fight with him. All desire for hurting, for recriminations seemed useless.

"I'm sorry I took up your bed," she said.

"I'm not."

"And I'll be gone in an hour, if that's all right with you."

He leaned across to the stove. "Would you like some coffee?" he said.

"Yes, thank you. I need it."

"Sit down. I'll pour."

She sat down, crossing her legs demurely beneath the long pajama top. "Why aren't you at the lab?"

He waited to answer till he'd set the cup on the table and pushed over the sugar bowl.

"The police phoned to tell me my wife had been through an ordeal and that I would be needed at home."

Carol's hands trembled in her lap. She did not move to lift the cup. "Then you've been here ..."

"Yes, ever since." He lit two cigarettes and passed one across to her.

"Then you saw Garril?"

"Yes."

"And Paterson?"

George smiled and pushed his glasses up on his nose. "How do you suppose they got in?"

"I didn't think of that," Carol said.

"Drink your coffee," George said, leaning his chair back against the wall.

Carol noticed how the top of his chair hit the black mark it had been making for the past seven years.

"Don't order me around, George," she said with hollow energy. "We're not playing at husband and wife any more."

"So I gather," he said. "Even though you did climb into my bed instead of your own when you got back here."

"That had nothing to do with you."

George took off his glasses and wiped them slowly on a paper napkin. "Seems nothing has anything to do with me."

"You have friends," Carol said, letting the bitterness show now.

"What does that mean?"

She remembered back to Tammy's phone call and the attempt at blackmail. "Well, Riker," she said. "He must have had plenty to say."

"He mentioned something."

"And Tom. Tom must have told you that I'm a raving lunatic."

He blew on one lens of the glasses and rubbed again with the napkin. "He told me some things, yes."

She watched the steam rising from her cup. She could just imagine what Riker had mentioned. And the way Tom must have shaped the course of events to suit his purposes. And for a moment she almost hated George, his complacency, his refusal to fight back. Why couldn't he...

"But," George continued, "I haven't heard your side of it yet."

"My side?" she said, startled.

"I presume you do have a version?"

Shaken and self-conscious, Carol remained silent. Then she remembered George's scientific background, the cautious approach with which he met life. Never draw any conclusions until all the facts are in.

"Who knows?" George encouraged. "Your view of it may even sound half-way sane."

"You mean Paterson's didn't?"

"I mean Paterson himself didn't."

A warm glow of gratefulness spread through her. He would listen open-mindedly, hear her out before he passed judgment. "George," she said softly, smiling.

"Just tell me the whole thing," he said.

Carol took a deep breath. "Well, I won't begin from the beginning," she said. "You know all that. But it all began to make a weird kind of sense to me later on."

"What did?" he said. "Maybe I don't know as much as you presume."

Carol smiled again. "I'm sorry," she said. "I'm just so full of everything that has happened. Anyhow, that night I went out with Jonny...the night of the party...someone was following him in a car. Someone was out to kill him. And when I recognized that car later on and they kept saying that it wasn't Garril's, I kept thinking about it till I remembered where I recognized it from. And how. It has a patched headlight, you see. And that's what I saw in the mirror, the headlights." She paused to reflect.

"Well, go on," George prompted.

"Well, then it was a question of why Paterson wanted to kill Jonny and why Jonny let him hang around anyway and when I spent that night with Garril, I realized from the way she behaved that she and Jonny must have been having an affair. I mean, Garril likes women, really. But even she fell for Jonny Chico. Everyone did sooner or later."

"I don't get it," George said. "What's that got to do with Tom wanting to kill Chico?"

"Don't you see," Carol said a little desperately. "Tom's in love with Garril. And all these years he's been thinking that the reason she turned him down was because she's queer. But if she had an affair with Chico and Tom knew it, then Tom would know ... or think, anyway ... that Garril had been kidding him along. And being the kind of man he is, he would be insanely jealous. And it makes perfectly good sense to me that he would want to kill the man who made out with Garril when he couldn't and——"

"Hey, wait a minute," George laughed. "Slow down a bit. I wasn't there, remember?"

Carol stopped in the middle of her sentence on a peak of breath. "No, of course you weren't," she said.

"But even an old slouch like myself can realize how far a man can go for money or jealousy or ... love," he said quietly.

Carol studied George's face and a wide stretch of calmness began to unfold within her. He wasn't making fun of her. He wasn't twisted with contempt or sneering at the nightmarish quality of her jumbled explanation.

*He believes me.*

"I'll tell it to you step by step," she said. "as far as I've been able to figure it out." She felt steady enough now to pick up her cup of coffee. "I think Paterson must have planned from the beginning to use Augusta as his means of murdering Jonny. I gather, from what he told the police, that he knew she was in the habit of walking out of the sanitarium and coming home for a visit now and then. And I'm positive he must have known that she was violent. My theory is that Jonny went to him for help one time when Augusta tried to commit suicide ... or murder, I don't suppose we'll ever know which. Paterson's money and influence could have saved Jonny a lot of embarrassment. And if what I think is true, then it would explain why Jonny couldn't just kick Paterson's teeth in when he realized that the man was after him. It would also explain—"

"Hey," George yelled suddenly as an overwhelming swoosh of water sounded to them through the rooms.

And they both ran for the tub that had spilled over.

Night had fallen again before Carol finished spewing the million details for George to see and appraise. They had returned to the kitchen, to the closed, cozy atmosphere where they had so often sat and spoken during the all too peaceful years.

Sandwich leavings and coffee cups and cigarette stubs piled high without concern. The ceiling bulb warmed and lit the small area high in the city's pattern of light and darkness.

When Carol had finished, her stomach and her chest ached. It was as though she had been vomiting for hours, ridding herself of a toxic substance.

"You know," George said seriously when she stopped speaking, "it sounds convincing enough to me because I know you. But I don't see how we can do a thing with it to strangers."

"Yes," Carol said, "that's the horrible part."

"But anyway," George continued, "can't we try? Even if we don't succeed, at least you'll know … and I'll know … that we did our best."

"Would you, George?" Carol's voice was low. "Would you spoil it for yourself and the lab? Would you give up the Paterson money on a gamble that can't possibly succeed?"

George shrugged. A touch of the old expansiveness crossed his face and straightened his shoulders. "You know what scientists are like, my dear. We're always willing to gamble on the absolutely impossible. That's how progress is made."

Carol said nothing. She stood up now and began clearing the kitchen debris. There was much to be done in the apartment to make it livable again, comfortable enough for two people to relax in.

Two people. Not three any more. After all these years, the subtle intrusion of Jonny Chico had ended. She had not realized before this that he had been a third partner to her marriage … that her memories of him had perverted her feelings for George, had tainted her reason, her enjoyment of life. She knew that the taint would remain with her for a long time to come. She would need help ... and love.

And George ... the husband who not only loved but trusted her ... was helping her now where she needed him most.

Carol turned to him.

"George," she said softly.

And for the first time in many years, she said it with appreciation.